# "You've Got To Stop Doing This."

"What?" he asked, his gaze moving to her mouth.

"You know what you're doing right now," Allison whispered. "We can't get close without—"

"Without steam rising," he finished.

"We weren't going to get personal. I can't. I'm on a job. Jared, cooperate. Think of my brother. That ought to cool whatever you're feeling."

"The last thing on my mind right now is your brother," he said in a raspy voice. He stepped back, and Allison should have felt relieved. Instead, her heart still raced and she wanted to flirt, to kiss him, to make love to him. Desire shook her.

She'd promised herself she'd get this job wound up so she could get away from temptation. But it was standing right in front of her. In the flesh.

\* \* \*

*One Texas Night...* is part of the Lone Star Legacy series: These Texas billionaires are about to get richer... in more ways than one

\* \* \*

If you're on Twitter, tell us what you think of Harlequin Desire! #harlequindesire

Dear Reader,

When handsome Jared Weston bumps into Allison Tyler, a tall, beautiful blonde with indigo eyes, he is immediately drawn to her. His interest deepens when he introduces himself, causing her to smile and call him the "forbidden man." From that moment on, the sparks fly between two people whose path to love often looks hopeless.

Against a Texas backdrop with glittering cities and elegant mansions, Jared and Allison deal with his inheritance from the Delaneys. These are two people who have known each other all their lives, yet don't really know each other in deep, meaningful ways until they fall in love. This story involves a handsome Texas mogul who realizes the wild, exciting pursuits in his life are not always the best thing. And Allison faces a choice: Can she take a chance and risk her heart for the man she loves?

This is another story involving a Delaney inheritance, a Lone Star Legacy with two strong, determined people who fall wildly in love. Thank you for your interest in this book.

Sara Orwig

# ONE TEXAS NIGHT...

—

## SARA ORWIG

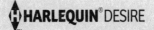

Recycling programs
for this product may
not exist in your area.

ISBN-13: 978-0-373-73279-1

ONE TEXAS NIGHT…

Copyright © 2013 by Sara Orwig

**Printed in U.S.A.**

www.Harlequin.com

## Books by Sara Orwig

### Harlequin Desire

**Texas-Sized Temptation #2086
**A Lone Star Love Affair #2098
**Wild Western Nights #2110
§Relentless Pursuit #2159
§The Reluctant Heiress #2176
§Midnight Under the Mistletoe #2195
The Texan's Contract Marriage #2229
Deep in a Texan's Heart #2246
§One Texas Night... #2266

### Silhouette Desire

Falcon's Lair #938
The Bride's Choice #1019
A Baby for Mommy #1060
Babes in Arms #1094
Her Torrid Temporary
  Marriage #1125
The Consummate Cowboy #1164
The Cowboy's Seductive
  Proposal #1192
World's Most Eligible Texan #1346
Cowboy's Secret Child #1368
The Playboy Meets
  His Match #1438
Cowboy's Special Woman #1449
^Do You Take This Enemy? #1476
^The Rancher, the Baby
  & the Nanny #1486
Entangled with a Texan #1547
*Shut Up and Kiss Me #1581
*Standing Outside the Fire #1594

Estate Affair #1657
Highly Compromised
  Position #1689
ΩPregnant with the
  First Heir #1752
ΩRevenge of the
  Second Son #1757
ΩScandals from the
  Third Bride #1762
Seduced by the
  Wealthy Playboy #1813
ΔPregnant at the
  Wedding #1864
ΔSeduced by the
  Enemy #1875
ΔWed to the Texan #1887
**Dakota Daddy #1936
**Montana Mistress #1941
**Wyoming Wedding #1947
Tempting the
  Texas Tycoon #1989
Marrying the Lone Star
  Maverick #1997
**Texas Tycoon's Christmas
  Fiancée #2049

^Stallion Pass
*Stallion Pass: Texas Knights
ΩThe Wealthy Ransomes
ΔPlatinum Grooms
**Stetsons & CEOs
§Lone Star Legacy

Other titles by this author
available in ebook format.

# SARA ORWIG

lives in Oklahoma. She has a patient husband who will take her on research trips anywhere, from big cities to old forts. She is an avid collector of Western history books. With a master's degree in English, Sara has written historical romance, mainstream fiction and contemporary romance. Books are beloved treasures that take Sara to magical worlds, and she loves both reading and writing them.

May God bless those in Oklahoma, as well as other storm-devastated areas, who have suffered loss and hurt. I pray and hope for blessings for you.

Also, a special thank you to Stacy Boyd.

# One

Though he was looking at his iPad, Jared Weston didn't see the notes he'd entered on the screen. He could only see the dark blue eyes, long blond hair and lush body that still took his breath away. After six years of endless struggles to fight the memories, he still hadn't forgotten a second of the night he had spent with Allison Tyler....

It had been at a June wedding reception at the then-new Houston country club. In the crowded ballroom, some-one had bumped him, causing a chain reaction. As he brushed shoulders with the woman beside him, champagne splashed from the crystal flute she held. A tall, willowy blonde, she wore a pale blue dress with a jacket cut high above her narrow waist. The dress ended inches from her knees, revealing long shapely legs.

He grabbed a flute of champagne from a passing waiter and held it out to her, taking the opportunity to look into her eyes. With thick lashes darkened slightly by mascara, her eyes were an unusual indigo-blue. He was momentarily riveted, feeling a sizzling attraction.

"I'm Allison Tyler," she said, smiling at him, taking the flute with one hand and offering the other.

As her hand settled in his, tingles emanated from the contact and he silently swore. Shocked, he focused more intently on her. She may look twenty, but she would be about eighteen now. Too young for him.

"That might be good news, and it might be bad news," he replied, shaking her hand, reluctant to release her, feeling as if he would lose her when he did and knowing that was exactly what should happen. Allison Tyler.

She cocked her head and asked, "Why?"

Her older brother, Sloan, was his lifetime best friend. Sloan was also the world's biggest worrier. Jared understood his friend's worrying. Since they had lost their mother and a brother, Chad, in a plane crash, Sloan had become far more cautious and protective of his younger sister.

Jared was torn between what he wanted and what he should do. "I think at this point, I should say goodbye," he admitted. When she gave him a confused look, he explained, "I'm Jared Weston."

Her eyes widened and her smile grew bigger as she laughed and tightened her hand on his, startling him. "The forbidden man. I should have recognized you instantly but it's been a few years." She stepped back slightly to give him room to view her from head to toe. "Guess what, Jared? I've grown up."

He looked at her...and he was captivated. Instantly. Of all the women on the earth, this was the sole woman he should avoid. So much younger than he was. His best friend's little sister. Why did she have to be so appealing?

"You have grown up. I didn't recognize you. You don't look at all like you did when you were seven or even twelve years old."

Her dark blue eyes sparkled with amusement. "Imagine that. I don't quite view you the same way I did then, either."

He realized then that her hand still rested in his.

"If we're going to hold hands, we might as well dance,"

he said. "One dance. I can't be a terrible influence in one harmless dance."

"Maybe it won't be so harmless," she said, flirting with him, sending his pulse racing faster.

"Allison, you're a temptation," he said, wanting to prolong the moment.

"Sloan does not run my life. We can dance if we want. Forget him."

Taking a sip of champagne, she set the flute beside his on a nearby table and joined him on the dance floor. When she stepped into his arms, her enticing scent enveloped him.

Looking at her, Jared could easily forget her older brother, his closest friend even now, although they saw little of each other any longer. "Do you still live at home in Dallas?" he asked, curious about her.

"Officially, but since I'm eighteen now and a freshman at the University of Texas, I'm in Austin."

"I'm twenty-four. Besides having Sloan's admonitions burned in my memory, I'm a lot older than you."

"An older man," she purred, those deep indigo eyes still twinkling. "That makes you all the more intriguing."

"You're a little on the naughty side, Allison," he said, smiling at her, trying to ease his conscience by telling himself a few dances were harmless.

"Well, isn't that more fun?" she asked, running her fingers lightly across the back of his hand. "I do not have to pay any attention to my overprotective brother, either. Since Mom died, he's been more a parent than my dad. And that's enough about Sloan. He's far away in Dallas, wrapped up in his own world."

"I have to pay attention to him. He's my best friend."

"Maybe I can make you forget that for a little while," she said in a mischievous tone, moving closer to him.

He had to laugh. "I think you already have. We're dancing, Allison, when I shouldn't be anywhere near you."

"I'm not scared of you or Sloan. Besides, you're having
fun, and this quiet, uneventful reception has suddenly become more interesting for both of us. You can't deny it."

"I can't possibly refute that," he said, tightening his
arm around her tiny waist. Was it because she was forbidden to him that he wanted her? She was a kid—a college
freshman—and he had finished college two years earlier.
He was too old for her, but she beguiled him. He wasn't
cutting short the dance or the evening.

"We're going to forget my brother. I'm of age, and I can
take care of myself."

He should have heeded that challenge and kept her
brother in his thoughts. Instead, he wiped Sloan clean out
of his mind. Even the undercurrent of guilt swiftly washed
away.

A fast number played next, and as they danced, she shed
the tiny blue jacket, revealing a tight spaghetti-strapped
dress that took his breath away. He wanted to unfasten
her updo, and impulsively he reached out and removed
the pins. A cascade of pale yellow-gold hair fell over her
shoulders, and his heart raced with excitement.

As she danced, her sexy moves fueled his fiery attraction. Whatever he felt, she gave indications she shared
the same sizzle.

They continued into the next dance—a ballad—and he
drew her closer this time. Her silky hair held a faint, inviting scent of jasmine and orange blossoms.

Slow dancing became a torment. Soft, warm, curva-
ceous in his arms, she fit perfectly against him. Her full
lips made him want to kiss her. How would she taste? How
would she respond?

During a break between dances, they sat on the darkened terrace, drinking champagne while they flirted with each other. How much of the night had been because of the effects of the champagne? He wished he could blame it all on the bubbly, but he knew he couldn't. A hot, intense attraction had flared the first moment they had looked into each other's eyes.

It was one o'clock in the morning when she said she should leave the reception and get back to her hotel room. He took her to her hotel, and they stopped in the bar for a drink. Within minutes they were headed to her room. The moment he closed her door, he reached for her, drawing her into his embrace while he leaned down to kiss her.

Wrapping her arms around his neck, she returned the electrifying kiss, which fanned desire to a blazing intensity. He had only planned on having a nightcap and then kissing her good-night, but his sensible plans were forgotten instantly. Instead, white-hot passion consumed him. She was as eager as he was. He wanted her as he had never wanted anyone before. Able to fight no longer, he surrendered.

Naked. Passionate. A virgin. All of those described the woman he took to bed. That she was innocent shocked him, briefly cooling his ardor, making him pause in their lovemaking. But then she wrapped those enticing legs around him and whispered a sigh in his ear and he was lost. He could never say no to her. So he made love to her, discovering a passionate woman and an ardent partner, whom he knew he'd never forget.

Later they showered together and made love again. The second time he took it slowly, with more than an hour of foreplay, trying to make it as great for her as possible by dedicating himself to pleasuring her.

She was like a flame, igniting his passion, burning it, until it finally devoured him, leaving him spent.

With the light of day, however, came reason.

They knew they could not see each other again because there was no future in it. Allison had college to get through. He had a career that was commencing, and they both had Sloan to contend with—a friend Jared did not want to hurt and a brother she wanted to keep happy.

So they agreed the night—the wonderful searing night—would be their secret.

He gave her a sweet, fleeting kiss goodbye at the door of her hotel room...and walked away....

Jared inhaled deeply. Wiping his brow as if to erase the memories that had haunted him for six years, he shoved away from his desk, the iPad notes long forgotten. With little provocation, he remembered that night with Allison as if it had happened yesterday. And he remembered her still.

They had never had contact again. Through the years, each of them had guarded the secret, kept their promises to never contact each other. He had seen her brother often at charity events, college football games, rodeos, occasional meetings if their businesses crossed paths and more recently in a breakfast club. But never in those encounters had he said a word to Sloan about Allison.

The last time he had seen Sloan, her brother had casually mentioned that she was thinking about marrying some guy. The news gave Jared a peculiar stab of pain that he shook off as ridiculous. She meant nothing to him. He had merely shared one night of passion with her. A night that was buried in silence, although never really forgotten.

Right now he could recall the entire night, moment by moment. His memory was flawless, he was sure, of making love to her, her passionate responses, her softness, her enthusiasm.

Jared walked to the window to look out at the sprawling city of Dallas as seen from the top floor of the Weston Energy building. Two flags in the distance fluttered in the March breeze. He wished it could blow away his memories just as easily.

But as he recalled the decision he'd made only days earlier, he knew there was no chance he'd be forgetting about Allison anytime soon.

He had just hired Tyler Antiques and Appraisals for a job he needed done and learned it would be Allison who would be doing his appraisal. In days the lover he'd never forgotten would be back in his life.

Thirty minutes later, composed, professional and looking slick in a custom suit, Jared walked into a downtown restaurant for a business lunch. He watched the youngest, tallest and the last unmarried Delaney approach their table from the opposite direction. He greeted Ryan, shaking hands with his friend, gazing at friendly dark brown eyes and an infectious smile.

"How's everything in Dallas?" Ryan asked.

"Everything is fine. How are your brothers?"

"Great. Will is being Will, still taking charge of the rest of the family. His wife is fine, and Caroline is crazy about her little brother."

"And your world-traveler brother? How does marriage suit him?"

Ryan grinned. "You won't know Zach. He's a desk jockey now. Goes to the office nine to five. He's retired from fieldwork and stays in the office. Very domestic. Phoebe is almost nine months old. She's a cutie."

"I can't imagine Zach sticking to an office. That's beyond me. I asked you to lunch so I could talk about my inheritance of the Delaney mansion in Houston."

"Talk away," Ryan said, sitting and picking up a menu.

As soon as they had ordered and the waiter disappeared, Jared leaned forward. "Ryan, it's your inheritance from your dad."

"I know that technically it's my inheritance, but it's because of our dads' friendship."

"Friendship and gratitude for the time our dads were both roughnecks, working in the oil patch. When that fire broke out on a rig, your dad saved my dad's life. The mansion is just a thank-you."

"I had nothing to do with any of that."

"Dad had it in his will that, if your dad is deceased, the mansion is to go to you. It's yours to do with as you please."

"One of the Tylers commences cataloging the contents of the mansion this week. Have any of you changed your mind about the mansion or its contents?"

"Absolutely not. I asked my brothers again, just for you, and they gave me the same answer. We don't want any part of the mansion. We never spent time there, and it's meaningless to all of us. Stop worrying about it. The mansion doesn't hold fond memories for any of us." Ryan reclined back in his chair, looking fully relaxed and filled with his usual self-confidence. "We inherited enough from Dad, and we're happy you have the mansion."

"It's a marvelous inheritance and I appreciate it."

"On the phone you said you'd hired Herman Tyler to do the appraisal. You have your own appraisal company now in addition to owning Weston Energy. Why hire Herman?"

"He's the best. I still have an offer to buy his business, merge it with mine and let him run his part, but he wants to keep it. Actually, I bought my appraisal company to try to entice Herman to run both and work for me, but he won't sell. I keep the offer open. Ryan, as far as the house and antiques are concerned, what about Sophia?" Ryan's half-sister was an artist. "I'd think she'd want some of the paintings."

"Will asked her, as well as Zach. That's not her type of art, and, no, she doesn't want any of it. None of us do."

"Even if I sell it?" Jared asked, intending to make certain no Delaney had regrets.

"If you didn't sell it, we would. Hear me," Ryan said, leaning in, "we do not want the mansion or its contents."

Jared put up his palms. "I'll take you at your word and drop the subject."

"Good. I'm riding in the Fort Worth rodeo later this month—bull riding. Are we competing again?" he asked, his eyes sparkling with devilment.

Jared had to grin. "We're competing, and I'm going to beat you."

"We'll see on that one," Ryan said, his lips twitching in a crooked smile. "Want to bet an extra hundred, plus a burger and a beer for the winner?"

"You're on," Jared said, enjoying the friendly competition he had with Ryan.

"I can't wait." Ryan tilted his head to study Jared. "You know, we're kindred souls."

"We both like life on the wild side."

"You're like I am—neither one of us wants to look back with regrets."

"Amen to that," Jared replied. "That's what my dad did."

When lunch was over, as Jared drove back to his office, he thought twice about his decision to involve Tyler Antiques and Appraisals in the Houston property. The call he had made to Mr. Tyler had not been what he had expected.

Jared hadn't mentioned Allison, so it had been a shock to hear from Herman that his daughter had taken over the part of the business that was conducted away from the office.

Allison Tyler still was the one woman on the whole planet that he did not want to get involved with. His long-time friendship with her brother was important to him. Too important to jeopardize. Sloan took a dim view of all the women in Jared's life and certainly would not want his sister to become one of them. Jared didn't want to be hounded by a threatening, hand-wringing big brother, which Sloan would be. Sloan also still thought Jared had a daredevil streak and risked his life constantly in wild pursuits.

His cell phone rang, and when he glanced at the caller ID, he saw it was Sloan. Feeling guilty as well as amused, he answered. "You didn't waste time," Jared remarked.

"Yeah, right. I talked to Dad just now. I heard you hired him to do some work for you."

"That's right. I've hired him before, and he does a great job."

"Thanks. I guess he told you that Allison will be the one to go to the site to inventory and catalog items, that sort of thing."

"Yes, he did."

"So you know why I'm calling. Women are drawn to you like ants to crumbs. And vice versa."

"I will not ask your sister out. Does that make you happy?" Jared said, having mixed feelings about Allison and knowing he was following the best course for everyone, himself included. "I've been seeing someone."

"That does not reassure me one degree. Whomever you're seeing will be gone six months from now."

Sooner than that, Jared thought but did not say. He had already broken it off with Dawn Rainsford, but Sloan did not need to know about the women in his life or lack thereof. "Nonetheless, you can save your breath. Your sister is there for a job. We will not socialize. I have my own life, and I'm not tangling with you over her. I do not want to lose my friend over his little sister. Actually, though, isn't she a grown woman now?"

"Very, but I'm still her brother and looking out for her best interests. I figure you're thinking about her and envisioning a ten-year-old kid who was a pest. I think the last time you saw her was at my wedding. She was fifteen. I don't want you hitting on her."

"This is a moot conversation, Sloan. I'm not interested."

"She's very pretty, and I know you far too well. Leave her alone. I don't want her heart broken by you."

"That will never happen."

"Is the movie star still in your life?"

"Definitely not. According to your dad, I'll only work with your sister a few days and then I'll be out of there and let her take over the liquidation. Just don't worry."

There was a stretch of silence that made Jared shake his head, but he hung on to his patience.

"Okay, Jared. She's busy, and she helps Dad, and she's dating a guy she'll marry. As a matter of fact, by now she's probably engaged to Phillip Blakely."

"I'm happy for her," Jared remarked drily. "How are you, Leah and the little Tylers doing?"

"We're great. You marry the right woman, Jared, and you can't imagine how happy you'll be. The kids are great. I hope the current woman in your life is the special one."

"Stop worrying, Sloan. See you at the next breakfast club."

When he ended the call, he wondered if they would repeat this conversation when they met with other businessmen for their monthly breakfast.

Jared shook his head again. Sloan was a fire-breathing dragon about his sister, which was absurd. Allison should be twenty-four now. Even at eighteen, she had been mature and her own person, capable of taking care of herself. Now

Sloan had a growing business of his own, as well as his kids to raise. He should let Allison go, but Sloan couldn't let anyone connected to him go. He hovered over Allison, and he probably hovered over his dad as well, ever since his heart attack, even though the man was now healthy and back to work.

For a brief moment when he had heard he would be working with Allison, Jared had thought about canceling, but he had worked with Tyler Antiques and Appraisals before, and Herman Tyler had been efficient with excellent expertise in the antiques business and the history of artifacts. Herman had been friendly and glad to have Jared's business, so Jared dismissed the thought of canceling as fast as it had come. He had gotten through a night with Allison. He could get through a couple of days of working with her at the Houston mansion.

He looked at his calendar. He'd get his secretary to cancel and rearrange meetings so he would be free for the next couple of weeks to go to Houston and stay if he wanted.

Had Allison changed in the intervening years? Had she ever thought about him? Had their night together been special to her? Questions were torment. If she truly was in love and engaged, as her brother indicated, Jared definitely had to forget her. But he could not avoid the curiosity. What was Allison like now?

# Two

Allison Tyler studied the small figurine in her hand, turning it to look at the initials and number on the underside. With her phone she took a picture that went first to her dad and then to her iPad. She made brief notes on her tablet. She was interested in getting a picture inventory, whatever descriptions she felt she needed and sending them on to her dad to do the research about each piece.

She'd battled mixed feelings since the first call to her father from Jared. The Delaney mansion Jared had inherited and wanted to sell was supposed to be filled with antiques and valuable art. It was a great job for them, just as it had been for her dad to work directly with him before. Jared had a hobby of deep-sea salvaging and twice had hired her father to go over items he had brought up from a find in the Gulf off the Alabama coast.

Jared. She couldn't stop thinking about him.

He'd been a constant companion of her brother's throughout their school years, but he'd been of little interest to Allison. Until six years ago when he had bumped into her at the wedding reception, and she'd felt as if a lightning bolt had struck her. He was incredibly handsome, sexy, appealing. She couldn't resist flirting with him. He'd set her heart pounding, and within the next hours, she'd decided he was the most exciting man she had ever met.

The night had been magical. Her brother had once told her that he didn't want his best friend around her. Though Jared was a great friend to Sloan, where women were concerned, Jared was totally unreliable. Sloan had described him as a playboy, a man who lived life on the edge, who liked mountain climbing, bull riding, white-water rafting, wild adventures and beautiful women.

At eighteen, when she had looked into Jared's vivid green eyes, she had been as drawn to him as a moth to flames. Exuding self-confidence, he had flirted, made her pulse race, and when he had kissed her, she had melted. No other kisses had been like his.

But the next morning, along with daylight, common sense set in. She couldn't get involved with a heartbreaker like Jared. She was just a college freshman. Her life was simple, safe and ordinary, and she wanted to keep it that way. Jared, on the other hand, was a risk taker. She never again wanted to go through getting the news that someone she loved deeply had been killed taking a risk. Like her mother, who had flown her small plane through a Gulf storm, killing herself and Chad in the crash. Allison never wanted to experience that kind of needless hurt again.

And there was Sloan. She suspected if Sloan knew about her night with Jared, it would end their long, close friendship. All she could do, then, was get Jared to agree they would not see each other again and the night had never happened.

She had since tried to forget him. It had been a struggle to forget someone as dynamic as Jared Weston. That night she had tossed her usual caution aside because he had been too handsome, too appealing, too exciting.

Now she was older and wiser, and she still felt Jared was a man to avoid. Currently she felt responsible for her dad, and she didn't want to cause him worry. In addition she had a running undercurrent of anger. Jared had tried to buy Tyler Antiques and Appraisals after her dad's heart attack. When her dad had refused to sell, Jared had bought another appraisal company and then approached her dad once more, wanting to merge the two, leaving her dad in charge of his part. Her dad loved his business that he had built, and he did not want to sell. Jared had said the offer would remain on the table. Her father never mentioned it again, and she hoped Jared was not now attempting to get their company.

In minutes, she forgot business when her thoughts returned to that night with Jared. How tempting would he be to her now? She suspected very tempting, because she had never been able to forget him. How appealing he was would not matter. He was still off-limits. Sloan had already told her that Jared was about to become engaged. That should keep distance between them.

She had arrived the previous day at the sprawling mansion in Houston. With very little landscaping, the gray three-story Gothic had a cold palatial appearance with medieval turrets, parapets and arched windows, and she could see why Jared intended to sell it. She couldn't imagine living in a home the size of the mansion, much less one so forbidding in appearance.

Jared had not arrived yet, and the housekeeper, Mrs. Tarkington, as well as the cook, who introduced herself only as Marline, were uncertain about exactly when he would arrive. Allison did not need Jared present to start an inventory of the art and furnishings. All she felt was relief that he was not here. By noon the first day, she had inventoried and tagged six rooms of furniture, sending brief descriptions and pictures to her father. She'd begun with the bedrooms so that they'd be done and she wouldn't have to deal with Jared in a bedroom—even if they were only remotely polite to each other. But she still had more bedrooms to complete, even after this one.

She paused in front of an ornate gilt-framed mirror to look at her image. It had been six years since she had seen Jared. How much would he think she had changed? How well did he remember that night? In six years she was certain it had been over and forgotten long ago for him. She took a critical study of her appearance: black slacks, a black cotton shirt, her hair secured on her head with a clip. Several blond tendrils had fallen around her face. She tucked them away and continued her inventory of antiques, moving to an upstairs sitting room.

In minutes a light knocking caught her attention and she turned. Looking as commanding and self-assured as she remembered, Jared stood in the doorway, leaning with one shoulder against the jamb. Her heart missed several beats as he smiled. Locks of wavy black hair framed his face. His spellbinding green eyes had not been an exaggeration of her memory. Six years ceased to exist. It could have been this past Saturday night that they had been together as far as her clarity of memory was concerned. A heart-pounding, unforgettable night of seduction. She thought her memories of him had dimmed, but she had simply fooled herself.

Her pulse raced and her physical reaction to him was far more intense than she had expected. Something she couldn't keep from happening. Dressed in a navy suit and matching tie and Western boots, he was breathtaking. She had a flashback, an instant memory of being naked in his arms, flush against his hard, muscled body.

"So how's it been for six years?" he asked, coming into the room.

She was thankful he couldn't detect her racing pulse. To her chagrin, her memory triggered heat that flushed her face. She hoped to look relaxed, to keep hidden all indications of her racing heartbeat.

"It's been busy, and I'm sure you can say the same. It's warm in here," she said, in an effort to explain her cheeks that had to be pink, because she could feel their warmth.

"I agree," he said in a huskier voice than she remembered, and she realized the next few days of working with him were going to be far more of a strain than she had anticipated.

*Strain or temptation?* a small inner voice taunted.

"I'll shed this jacket," he said, shrugging it off and draping it on a chair. His tie followed, and he unfastened the top buttons of his snow-white shirt. Her insides tightened. She could imagine him peeling away the shirt. He turned to face her again.

Reaching out, he caught her left hand and turned it in his. "I don't see an engagement ring. Sloan said you'd be engaged."

She laughed, relaxing slightly. "My dragon brother, who thinks he is protecting me, still sees you as the wild man. No, I'm not engaged," she replied, catching a flicker in the depths of his green eyes. She was amused and annoyed slightly with her brother, but not surprised. Attempting to focus on their conversation, she tried to ignore the warmth of Jared's hand, his thumb lightly brushing back and forth over her knuckles. A faint touch, yet scalding. She had all the compelling reactions to him that she'd had that first night, now more disturbing because of the hours of passion with him. "Sloan is still protective even though I'm twenty-four and capable of taking care of myself."

"I think I'm the one Sloan is trying to manipulate here," Jared replied. "He still wants me to keep away."

"He said you're almost engaged."

Jared's perfect white teeth flashed in a grin, while he

shook his head. "Your rascal brother. No, I'm not about to become engaged. Not even close."

"I should have guessed," she said. She knew she should get them back to a professional discussion, but she was too tempted to flirt with him as she had that magical night. She forced herself to withdraw her hand from Jared's. "This mansion is filled with treasures."

"Take a break and let's get a cool drink and talk about what I would like your company to do."

Was there a streak of disappointment that he was also being professional? "Of course," she said as she nodded. She would get directions, and then he could stay out of her way. She would tag the things to sell and get ready to list them in a brochure for their clients. With her father doing the research, she should be able to get a complete inventory in two to three weeks at a maximum.

"Sure. It's better I hear the directions from you rather than from my dad secondhand."

"You could have called me," he said lightly, startling her for an instant until she realized he was referring to the directions.

"I figured I would see you here and could get the info. Why did you hire my dad when you have your own company now?" she asked bluntly.

"Your dad is the best. I'm happy to have my own company, and it's good, but your dad is the best I've ever worked with."

"Thank you. I think so, too," she replied coolly, thinking about Jared's desire to buy her father's company. "Dad loves the business, and he intends to keep running it as long as his health holds."

"That's great. So what's happened in the years between?" he asked again as they strolled down a wide hall filled with statues and oil paintings in ornate frames. The mansion was beautiful, but silent and empty of life, reminding her of a museum.

"I graduated from college, did an internship at a museum and then was hired by a different museum. After a year I went to work with Dad, and last year he had a heart attack. He was told to sell the business, something he didn't want to do in spite of your offer. So I took over the fieldwork and let Dad stay in the office."

"Sorry to hear all that. Your dad is good at what he does. I liked working with him."

"It's mutual. And so far, it's working out well," she said, aware of Jared close beside her as they descended the wide front stairs to the main hall. "What have you done in the intervening years?"

"More of the same—what I was doing when we met. I have Weston Energy that I took over after my dad died and a few other smaller businesses that I've bought. Plus I follow my interests."

"Sorry about you losing your dad. He would be very proud of you now, because Weston Energy has become a lot larger since you took over," she said, knowing the company had been small all the years his dad had ran it, but when Jared had stepped in at his father's death, it had grown swiftly into a huge conglomerate. "With your dad gone, that leaves you alone, doesn't it?"

"I have three aunts. Mom died two years before Dad. She had a heart problem. Otherwise I'm it now."

"So you inherited this mansion from the Delaney family."

"Yes. My father and Argus Delaney started out together as roughnecks in the oil patch. Both were successful. Dad died before Argus, but Argus already had him in his will. He was always grateful to my dad. I heard Mr. Delaney tell the story a dozen times about how my father saved his life in a well fire. This mansion was to go to my dad, but since he is deceased, it's mine now."

"The whole place is filled with beautiful things, very old, I imagine some very rare," she said, following the conversation but still more conscious of him beside her, close enough she could detect a hint of his aftershave. The work would be easy once he departed, but being near him was even more disturbing than she had thought it would be.

"I don't want them all. Some I like and will keep. As for the others—I don't know which are valuable and which are merely nice, but of little lasting worth. That's partially why you're here," he said.

"Dad and I will inventory the contents. I'm taking pictures of everything for the catalog that will show what you want to sell. You'll see it first, of course, and you can let me know what you want to keep."

"I have a better idea," he said, leading her to a terrace where he motioned her to an outdoor kitchen and dining area. "I'll go around the place with you and we can talk about what I like, what's extremely old and valuable, that sort of thing."

"That may make this inventory process take longer," she said, contemplating the hazards of working constantly with him.

One dark eyebrow arched. "You can't do that?"

"Of course I can. I'm just telling you," she said, trying to sound matter-of-fact despite her alarming pulse rate. The thought of having him beside her constantly for the next two weeks or more was way too appealing.

His gaze became intense. "You don't want to work with me?"

"We can work together. I'm just telling you the job may take a little longer that way."

"That's all right. If I'm here to tell you what I like, we

won't have misunderstandings. Now we've got that settled, what would you like? Iced tea? Coffee? Soda pop?"

"Tea is fine," she said, perching on a bar stool to watch him get two tall glasses of iced tea. "I can see why you wouldn't want to keep this palatial mansion. Do the Delaney heirs mind that you inherited it?"

"I'm closest with Ryan Delaney, and he's assured me that they don't at all. They inherited enough themselves that they're happy, and Ryan said none of them ever spent time at this place, so it holds no sentimental value for them. His dad got this mansion in a business deal. The previous owners settled a debt by deeding him this place. I'm the fortunate one," he said, his thickly lashed green eyes making it difficult to pay attention to what he was telling her.

"There are some things I like, and some I'm uncertain about. I'll show you pictures of my two houses, and you tell me what you think will fit in and look nice. Otherwise I want to sell the mansion and everything inside it. I've told the Delaneys to come get what they want first, but they've all indicated they'll pass."

"Then they really don't want any of this," she said.

"No, Ryan said they don't. I plan to sell the furnishings and art separately from the mansion because I think you and your dad can get me a better deal."

"I'm glad you made that decision," she said lightly.

"I like some of the old furniture, like the beds in your room and mine."

"I haven't seen yours, but the one in my suite is solid oak and so well preserved. I'm guessing eighteenth-century France," she said. "I've done most of the bedrooms, but I still have four to go."

"I'll show you mine anytime you want to see it," he said with a faint smile.

"That's an offer I'll keep in mind," she couldn't resist

answering, remembering what fun it was to flirt with him.
"I'll work downstairs for now," she added, trying to get
back to a professional level.

"Anytime. I'm always available."

"I can imagine." She suspected he did remember that
night when she had been eighteen.

"Shall we?" He motioned toward an adjoining sunroom
that overlooked the lit veranda and pool area. As she sat,
he pulled his chair close to hers to sit beside her, getting
out his phone. "Here is my Dallas home," he said, leaning closer so she could view the picture on his cell phone
with him.

"Your Dallas mansion looks as large as this place, if not
larger," she said, aware again of their shoulders and arms
touching. She looked up to meet his gaze as he flipped to
another picture.

"Might be. It's what I like, so I don't view it as huge.
It's more appealing to me than this place. This one has a
cold, remote look to it." He switched to the next picture.
"Here are the rooms."

She agreed about the cold appearance of the gray mansion, but she didn't mention it. They went through some
pictures of rooms in his Dallas home, and then he switched
to pictures of a lavish ranch home in Wyoming.

"I think the best I can do for you is get everything inventoried and perhaps make some suggestions. I'm not an
interior decorator, but I can try at least. I'll need pictures
of these rooms to study more thoroughly."

"Sure. Now I'd like to go through the house with you
and tell you which things I like and what I want to keep.
Actually, what I'd really like to do—"

Smiling, she bent forward quickly to place her fore-
finger lightly on his lips to silence him. The instant she
touched him, she removed her finger as a current sizzled

to her toes. It had been a mistake to touch his mouth, but she couldn't take it back.

"So would I, but it would be unprofessional and not the smart thing to do. Let's stick to business," she said breathlessly, lost again while looking into his eyes and besieged by memories.

Looking amused, he nodded. "Maybe I don't have on my mind what you think I do," he said.

"Maybe not, but just in case you do, prevention is better."

He grinned. "We can have fun."

"Stick to business," she said, wishing she could sound positive and forceful.

"You're all grown up. No flirty college girl now."

"I'm trying not to be," she answered, thinking that was the last thing she needed, if she was to work with him the next several days. "So we'll stick to getting items you want to sell separated from the ones you want to keep and get all the contents cataloged. We can start as soon as you want."

"Start which?" he asked with a twinkle in his eyes.

"C'mon, Jared. Let's stick to business."

"All right. I guess that's the wisest course for both of us, but it's definitely not the most exciting or the most fun."

She couldn't help feeling a bit disappointed that he had stopped flirting with her. She wondered whether they would be together constantly. The whole prospect of this job had changed, turning everything topsy-turvy, with work becoming a secondary consideration.

"Perhaps we should start now," she said, smiling at him and taking a long drink of tea. She set down the glass and stood. "I'll work downstairs this afternoon," she said, wanting to avoid the bedrooms anytime he was around.

"Sure." He rose to walk with her. One of the front rooms was a library, where he stopped in front of the painting nearest the door. "Here's something I want. I think this can go in the Wyoming ranch house."

She looked at the oil painting of a mountain stream with horses nearby. "You're not a contemporary fan. You like the traditional. That's a marvelous painting," she said, making more notes. While she placed a small sticker on the back of the painting, Jared strolled slowly around the room.

"I like that table," he stated, pointing to a Queen Anne–style mahogany table.

"Again a good choice in my opinion, but I love the sort of art and furniture here," she stated, making her notes and tagging the underside of the table.

He rolled back his sleeves, and they worked together. She took pictures and narrated descriptions, which Jared typed into her iPad. As they moved around, Jared told her what he wanted. When they finished the library, they moved to a study.

She lost consciousness of time, but never of him. She was too aware of his proximity, too filled with vivid memories that tormented her. He picked up a porcelain figurine of a hunter and dog. Turning it in his hand, he looked at it for seconds and then held it out to her. "Is this piece old? Valuable?" Her fingers brushed his as she accepted it, feeling the warmth of his hand yet the cool, smooth touch of the porcelain. The physical contact with him, while slight, stirred a shower of sparks. She remembered his hands, their texture, the calluses, their magic touches as they moved over her.

Jared worked through the rest of the afternoon with her, finding treasures, discarding things he didn't care for. He kept everything as professional as possible, just the way she had asked.

Finally he glanced at his watch. "Enough for today.

Let's take a break, meet in thirty minutes in the family room for a drink and then we'll have dinner."

She was startled to see it was already six o'clock. "That's fine."

"I told my housekeeper to take you to your suite of rooms, and I hope you had a chance to get a little settled in."

"Mrs. Tarkington did show me my rooms. I can settle in after dinner."

He smiled. "I can help if you'd like."

"Thanks. I'll manage on my own."

"Maybe after dinner we'll sit and talk a little."

"Perhaps," she said, aware that socializing with him would be difficult to avoid.

"I'll go change now, too. And show you where I'm staying." He took her arm, another light touch that caused a deep reaction. Would these volatile reactions fade or grow more intense the longer they were together? She suspected the latter.

"Have you already sent the information you gathered today to your dad?"

"Yes, most of the information and pictures. Not all. I'll go over the rest tonight after dinner."

"You have a small desk in your suite, and you have Wi-Fi and a laptop if you should need one."

"Thank you. I have my own," she said, climbing the steep, straight staircase beside him. When she reached the suite she had been given, she turned and looked into his green eyes that continued to keep her pulse racing. His thick lashes made his eyes irresistibly seductive.

"My suite is next to yours, so I'll be close should you need anything."

"I'll be fine," she said, turning to enter her suite.

"Meet you on the veranda," he said before she closed the door.

Were they going to eat together often? For some reason she remembered him saying he wasn't engaged. Or even verging on it. "It doesn't matter," she whispered to herself. He still had the wild lifestyle he always had. She had heard her brother talk about the reckless things Jared liked to do—mountain climbing, skydiving, hang gliding. Unfortunately Jared made her heart pound and her breath catch, and no other man ever had.

She needed to finalize this inventory and get back home. Too much time with Jared was a temptation to danger.

Just seeing him brought back memories of their night together. A night that still stirred her desire and made him far too appealing. A night that remained vivid and held too many scalding memories. Jared was as sexy as ever. He didn't flirt as much and neither did she, but she could feel the heat, the attraction, and she suspected he could, too.

Could she get through the next few days with him without a kiss? That might have to be her goal as much as cataloging the inventory. She wanted to get this job completed and return to her quiet world where there was no Jared Weston to tempt her. No matter how appealing and exciting Jared was, Allison didn't want to get so deeply involved with him that she cared. With a man like Jared, life would be a continual roller coaster.

Hurrying to dress for dinner, she wore a short green cotton skirt, a matching cotton blouse and flat sandals. She twisted and braided her hair, fastening it on her head, hoping to look cool and remote, and to keep things that way between them through dinner.

When she stepped outside, Jared turned to greet her. Dressed casually now in chinos and a black knit shirt, he still took her breath away. The evening presented a challenge the minute she saw him.

As she approached him by the pool, he walked toward her, his look of approval warm while he smiled at her. "You look great." When his gaze lingered on her mouth, her pulse drummed.

"Thank you. I brought my iPad and thought we might get one more room done after dinner tonight."

His smile broadened. "Sure, if you'd like," he said, taking the iPad from her to place it on a table. "In a hurry to get through and get away?" he asked, walking closer to her. "Scared of me? Or taking your brother's warnings seriously now? Or something else?" he added, studying her.

"I'm trying to stick to business," she answered, her heart racing beneath his piercing gaze. His green eyes ignited memories of his mouth on hers, his tongue, his taste. The hot need for more then, as now, became a temptation to reach for him. She was fighting memories of his kisses that still could make her tingle merely thinking about them.

"Ever hear of stopping work for the evening?"

"I think sticking to business is a far safer course to follow."

"Safer than being with me? I'm dangerous?" he asked, his dark eyebrows raising slightly. "How am I a threat? Boyfriend at home? What about Phillip? Your brother said you're almost engaged. Is your brother wringing his hands until you're away from me? What is it?" Jared asked.

"No boyfriend," she said, barely able to recognize her own voice that had become breathless. "Phillip and I are old and close friends, that's all. And I don't have to answer to Sloan. He's got his family, and I'm an adult now."

"So what does that leave?" Jared prompted, his voice becoming deeper and his gaze intensifying, making her breathing difficult.

"That you're an incredibly sexy, appealing man who might be a bit of a threat to my quiet life. You're definitely not ready to settle down, whereas I have reached the point in my life where I'm more interested in long-term, serious relationships or none at all. Does that answer your question?" she asked, gazing up at him. Her heartbeat raced as she watched him. Her words should put up a wall between them, make him stop and think before he flirted or touched her.

"After that description, if you expect me to back off and become all business and purely professional—" He paused to shake his head and move still closer, resting one hand lightly on her shoulder, his fingers playing back and forth slowly on her nape, a sensitive, erotic part of her. "It isn't going to happen," he finished. She heard his words while his touch immobilized her. *"Incredibly sexy,"* he repeated in a hushed tone, leaning toward her. "I'm not going away when you tell me that's how you see me."

She placed her hand on his chest to stop him from coming any closer. Her heart pounded while she looked up at him and the tension between them heightened. As his gaze lowered to her mouth, it was impossible to draw in enough air to breathe. The urge to lean toward him strengthened, creating another inner battle.

"You may not be going away, but I'm not coming any closer in spite of my description. I'm here to do a job. I intend to do it and then go home and forget all about you again."

A faint smile tugged up one corner of his mouth as he stepped close and slipped an arm around her waist. "I don't think you've ever forgotten. Right now I think you recall that night as clearly as I do. I remember how soft you are," he said in a voice that dropped and grew thicker. "I remember how passionate you can be—"

Her heart pounded while desire consumed her even as she placed her fingers on his mouth to stop him from talking. He kissed her fingers, his tongue touching them, and she yanked her hand away and wriggled out of his embrace.

"We get back on an impersonal basis, or I eat dinner elsewhere," she threatened.

"We can do whatever you want," he said, stepping away. "But sometime soon we'll do what I want. We could make a wager on that one. A wager I would win." He turned to walk toward the bar. "What would you like to drink tonight?" he asked, stepping behind the bar to face her. "We have everything. Fully stocked. What's your pleasure?"

His transformation had been far swifter than hers. She still burned with desire and struggled to think of business and to get Jared out of her thoughts. She wanted to return to a purely business relationship, wanted to maintain an impersonal one tonight. "I'll have a piña colada," she said, naming the first drink that came to mind.

She climbed onto a bar stool to watch him mix drinks. His well-shaped hands moved with efficiency, stirring her memories of his hands on her body, her legs, moving over her, creating magic. Inhaling a shaky breath, she shifted her attention to the swimming pool with a waterfall and three fountains. All except the pool were dry, turned off since the mansion was no longer lived in, she assumed.

"Are you busy with jobs like this one all the time?" he asked.

"Not at all. We have sales. There's always inventory to keep track of, billing, office stuff. If I have a chance, which is rare, I spend time studying antiques, their history, the different styles of furniture, art history. I'm amazed by how much my dad knows. This is a fascinating field," she said, thinking the most fascinating thing in her life at the moment was the tall, dark-haired man she faced.

"So you like what you do," Jared said, coming around the bar to hand her a drink while he held his. "Let's go sit where it's a little more comfortable," he suggested before she could answer him.

"Yes, I love this work. Sloan will never go into this line of work, but I want to help my dad and help grow the business," she replied as Jared directed her toward a grouping of outdoor furniture. When she sat, he pulled his chair close, turning slightly to face her.

He raised his drink. "Here's to success," he said.

She had to smile. "I'll drink to that," she said, raising her glass and taking a sip. "Even though you didn't specify what endeavor you had in mind with this toast."

"Care to try to guess what's on my mind?"

She laughed. "I don't think so. I've told you what I want. What do you want in your future?"

"Made you laugh. That's good," he said. "What do I want in the future?" he repeated. "In the near future—tomorrow night—I want to take you to dinner."

"Thank you, that would be nice," she said, deciding not to fight him at every turn.

"'Nice' sounds a little dull."

"'Nice' sounds absolutely perfect to me. A simple dinner out."

"Good. Half past six. We'll go early because I'm anxious."

She had to smile again. "I doubt if you've been 'anxious' over a woman since you were ten years old."

"You may have the wrong impression, which hopefully I'll change."

"I don't believe you need to give one second to that endeavor. It's unnecessary," she said. Wanting to change the subject, she steered their talk back to their work. "As far as the furnishings are concerned, so far, the oldest piece I've found in this house is a sixteenth-century chest." He evidently caught on to her intention, because he couldn't hide a smile.

"Let's forget the inventory and business for the evening," he said. "In a way, we know each other intimately. In another way, we barely know each other at all. I know your family. Your brother is my best friend, and your dad has worked with me on two projects. But you are a mystery. Besides the business, what do you want in life? You've told me that you like the business and want to see it grow, so I assume you'll stay in it as long as it's successful."

"That's right. At least that's what I plan now, and Dad needs my help," she replied, aware Jared gave her his full attention. "I want to marry, have a family, lead the same kind of life I had growing up. Isn't that what you want?"

"I like life's challenges. My dad did, and maybe that's where I got that need. I watched him spend a lifetime putting off the risky things because he was a husband, a dad, a businessman with a growing company. Then when he could retire and do the things he had dreamed of all his life, his health was gone and he couldn't do any of the adventures he had postponed. It was sad. He was filled with bitterness and regret," Jared said, his gaze shuttered as if looking back into the past. "I lost Mom two years before Dad. I don't know if she had things she wanted to do that she'd never done. She never said."

For the first time Allison didn't think she had any of his attention. She wanted no part of the lifestyle he craved, but she could understand a little better his reasons for choosing it.

"My brother never felt that way, yet he used to do some of the things you do."

"Sloan has a zest for life. He did things and satisfied himself about them, and now he doesn't live that way. He's settled. His choice. That's better than the way my dad lived, filled with regret. I don't want that to happen to me. I want to do all those things while I'm young."

"Even though it means you'll stay all alone in life?" she asked. "You might be missing out on the best parts of life and will have as many regrets later as your dad, just different regrets."

"I don't intend to be alone all my life. As for a family for me? I see that sometime in the distant future. I have things I want to do, and it's better to be single to do them. At least that's what I think. Climb Mount Everest, for one. Look how Sloan's life has changed since his marriage. Your brother has dropped out of the rodeo circuit. At one time he wanted to climb Everest with me. He's out of that now. Your brother is a family guy, which is good for him. I'm just not there yet."

"That's an honest answer," she replied.

"And I'd like to do more with salvaging. I've already explored two sunken ships and brought up artifacts that are in museums, and some treasures that are in my own collection. I'm sure you know that's when I worked with your dad. Salvaging is my most fascinating pursuit, and I'd like to spend more time doing it." He sipped his drink.

"And I'm still riding the rodeo. In fact, I'm riding in one in Ft. Worth soon." He put his drink down and leaned toward her. "Go to the rodeo with me. You used to go with your family to watch your brother."

She moved back impulsively. "Thank you, but I'll be in Dallas and back in my world by then. When I leave here, we won't see each other again. It'll be like the past six years. We each have our own lives."

"It's just a rodeo, Allison. You weren't this skittish with me before," he observed.

"Life's different now. Before we were at a party. I wasn't on a job. I worry about my dad and don't want to be away long periods of time or cause him any worry."

"Your dad isn't going to worry because you're watching me in a rodeo."

"He might worry because I'm out with you."

Her words seemed to have no effect on him. He persisted, "I doubt if Sloan has painted such a dark picture of me to your dad."

"I know he hasn't, or Dad would have never sent me on this job. My dad thinks you're a fine person. Sloan keeps those warnings about you for me—only since he found out I'm taking this job."

"I've worked with your dad, too, remember? We got along great."

"I'm sure you did."

"Your dad has always been nice to me." He sat back, his drink in his hand again. "You think about the rodeo. For now, tell me about all the furniture. What happens after you've tagged it?"

She went over the process once again, describing their work in detail, all the while conscious of his total focus.

They talked through dinner, through watching the sunset and finally they moved inside to talk more about various topics.

She had relaxed at last, finding him fun to be with, and she could see why her brother was close friends with him.

It was one o'clock in the morning when she finally told him that she had to turn in. He walked her to her suite, pausing outside her door.

"Good night, Jared," she stated. "Dinner was great, and

it's been a nice evening. You know, I could work in the evenings, too, and get finished sooner."

"No, no, you should have some time off. There's no big rush on this. You'll get it done." He smiled at her. "I enjoyed tonight, too. I'm looking forward to tomorrow night," he said in a deeper voice.

Her heart beat faster. He stood close, his gaze drifting slowly over her. She wanted to look at his mouth, to lean closer and press her lips to his. She could all but taste his kiss. "Tonight was enjoyable. I'm sure I'll see you in the morning," she said, turning, expecting his hand to touch her any minute. Instead he merely stood there while she entered her suite and closed the door.

Disappointment enveloped her despite knowing it was best they did not kiss. Her lips tingled. Her skin was hot, prickly with wanting him. She should be relieved they were sticking to business. If only her body would get that message.

# Three

Sleep was long in coming. And when it did, it was filled with so many dreams of Jared, Allison felt relieved to wake and see the room filled with the gray light of dawn.

She showered, dressed in pale yellow slacks and a matching shirt and went down to breakfast. Before she reached the bottom of the stairs, Jared appeared. He had been swimming. Bare chested, wearing black-and-white swim trunks with a towel over his shoulder, he paused to look up at her and her breath left her; her heart thudded against her ribs.

Instantly memories bombarded her—his broad shoulders, his sculpted chest, his body of hard planes and muscles. Recalling her mouth drifting over him, her hands exploring, touching, his body against hers… The visions came like tormenting ghosts. Her mouth went dry, and she forced in a deep breath.

She was afraid he could hear her heart pounding. "Morning swim?" she asked, her words little more than a whisper.

"Yes. I swim every morning that I can. Even though the fountains and waterfall are turned off, I've kept the pool heated, cleaned and treated. Hereafter you can join me. I didn't think to tell you last night."

"Thanks, but I'm not a morning swimmer. It has to be very hot weather to drive me to swimming."

"Then you've changed. I seem to remember you in the pool every time Sloan and I would swim at your house."

"It just seemed that way because in your eyes I was a nuisance back then," she said, making an effort to keep her gaze on his face and not look at his naked chest again.

He grinned. "I don't ever recall saying you were a nuisance."

"Actually, you just paid no attention to me. I might as well have not existed."

"And now look at you—not a kid anymore and not the least bit a nuisance," he said, his gaze drifting slowly over her and making her warm from head to toe.

"I'm going to get breakfast. I'll see you later," she said, and then dragged her eyes away as she strode past him.

He placed his hand lightly on her arm and she looked up sharply. His faint touch triggered more scalding memories. In her peripheral vision she was fully aware of how close he stood, how little he wore. "I'll be there as soon as I shower and dress," he said. His words were harmless; his deep tone was not.

The pounding of her heart was loud in her ears. Nodding to Jared, she went down the stairs. At the foot of the steps, against good judgment, she glanced back. Standing at the top, he looked down at her. He turned, giving her a glance at his smooth back that tapered to a narrow waist, his firm butt and long muscled legs. Every inch of him embedded itself in her memory.

She couldn't help but want this job to be over quickly so she could return to her quiet life. But just a glance at Jared in all his half-naked glory had her hot, riddled with desire. She could have an affair with Jared, couldn't she? But that was all it would be. An affair. An affair that would, ultimately, break her heart. He would never be serious—about her or any woman. He'd said as much just last night when he had listed all the wild, adventurous things he wanted to do. She told herself that even one night with him was a risk she didn't want to take. But then she remembered his kisses—and she realized Jared Weston was temptation personified.

She shook her head as if to dislodge the threatening thoughts and walked into the kitchen.

The ultramodern kitchen boasted dark granite countertops, stainless-steel appliances, a polished hardwood floor, dark cabinets and crown molding. Someone, she noticed, had already made coffee, and a pitcher of cold orange juice was on the counter.

She busied herself washing blueberries, washing and cutting strawberries. She turned to find Jared standing in the doorway.

"You have a way of quietly appearing," she said, trying to ignore the buzz her system experienced at the sight of him.

"Just watching you work," he said, coming into the kitchen. Her mouth became dry as he crossed the room to take the knife from her hands and place it on the counter. His tight jeans and navy knit shirt stretched against his sculpted muscles, giving him a more sensual appearance. As she looked up, she was barely aware of what he was doing because she was lost in his green eyes.

"Go sit and I'll do this," he said, without making a move to do anything. He stood too close to her, and their locked gazes made her pulse drum.

"I can help with breakfast," she said, her voice sliding to a whisper. She looked at his mouth and remembered his kisses. "Jared," she said as she realized she was moving slightly toward him and—

She caught herself just in time before she did something she'd regret. She moved away quickly. "You go right ahead," she said, turning to sit at the oval oak table. When she faced him, she was surprised to find him standing where she had left him, still watching her.

Even as he stood there without moving or talking, his dynamic presence seemed to fill the room. Desire was tangible, electric.

Finally he broke the moment. With a flick of his eyes, he turned to wash his hands.

His back to her, she looked freely. Her gaze ran over the length of him, remembering how he had looked only a short time earlier when he had worn just swim trunks.

"This is ridiculous for me to sit and watch. Let me help you." She got up and went back, this time careful to keep a safe distance between them.

She poured two cups of coffee and placed them on the table. She returned to get glasses for juice. Before she realized it, he had hemmed her in, placing his hands around her on the counter. "Go sit and relax. I'll get breakfast."

"You've got to stop doing this," she said.

"What? Fixing breakfast?" he asked, his gaze moving to her mouth. She could barely breathe.

"You know what you're doing right now," she whispered. "We can't get close to each other without—"

"Without steam rising," he finished, meeting her gaze again.

"We weren't going to get personal. I can't. I'm on a job, and I don't want to go home and send my dad here, because he's not physically able to do this any longer. Jared, cooperate. Keep in mind I want marriage in my future. That ought to cool whatever you're feeling."

She gazed into inscrutable eyes that held hers captive.

"I don't want you unhappy," he said.

"If we stick to business, I won't be."

"I'm having some trouble with that."

"Then…think of Sloan. Anything."

At the mention of her brother, Jared stepped back a fraction. "The last thing on my mind right now is your brother," he said in a raspy voice.

As Jared stepped farther away, she also put a few feet between them. She should feel relieved. But her heartbeat still raced, and she wanted to go back to flirting with him, to kissing, to making love again.

She moved automatically, getting dishes to set the table, pouring juice for them while he scrambled eggs. She dropped bread into the toaster, but her thoughts were still on Jared, her gaze running down the length of him when his back was turned. Desire shook her, and vivid images tormented her.

She promised herself she would work as efficiently as possible to get this job wound up so she could get away from the temptation.

Finally she sat across from him, too aware of each brush of their fingers as they passed dishes back and forth until they both had plates with toast and fluffy scrambled eggs.

"I've been thinking about it, and what I'd like to do is take you to see my homes in Dallas and Wyoming, and then you can help me decide what to put in them. How about that?"

Surprised, she paused, lowering her orange-juice glass to the table. "Once again, I'll say that's out of my area of expertise." However, she couldn't help thinking how much more her family business would make if she did what Jared was asking.

She hedged, saying, "I think for a task like that, you need a professional decorator."

"I don't want a decorator. I want your opinion on these

old things. You know what's valuable and what isn't. You'll know where furniture and art will fit and where it won't. And by fit, I mean look right. You have good taste, or you wouldn't be in this business."

"But that's all it would be. My taste. My opinion."

"I understand, and that's what I want. I trust your judgment on this."

"You don't even know me, and you've never seen where I live. You don't know my tastes."

"Yes, I do. I know Sloan. I know your dad. I know what the house you grew up in looks like. I have great faith in you on this matter."

"Thank you for the vote of confidence," she remarked drily. "Let me think about it. That's a whole different job from what I'm doing now." It also meant being with him at least three times longer than she would be if she refused to accept the job. Could she work that closely with him that much longer?

"If it helps make up your mind, I will triple the amount I'm paying you now."

She gazed at him in silence, still debating what to do. If she could resist Jared's charm, the job would be a boon for their business. And it would make her father happy— as long as she didn't get involved with Jared.

"You're worried about us getting involved, I know. We're adults, and we can avoid it if that's what you want."

She kept her voice even, though her pulse was racing again. "Avoiding an affair is definitely what I want, and that's the stumbling block here."

"Seems simple to me. Just keep it all business."

"Since when have you kept anything all business with me?" she couldn't keep from asking, biting back a laugh, which made him smile in return.

"With only minor exceptions, I think I've been doing a

grade-A job of sticking to business. For a few minutes I can show you the difference, and then you'll agree with me."

"I already know the difference, so stick to business."

"And that's what you want?" he asked. He sat back in his chair, one foot propped on his other knee. He looked relaxed, as if pleased with the way things were going between them. For all his carefree manner, he was paying close attention to whatever she said.

"Definitely."

"Somehow I get the feeling—"

"Definitely, Jared," she repeated, more slowly.

She wanted an impersonal relationship, and she wanted his business. For triple her fee, she'd take the risk.

She stuck her hand out for a shake, the consummate professional. "We have a deal, Mr. Weston. As long as you fully understand that I haven't done this before and am out of my area of expertise."

"I'm certain you'll do a great job." He shook her hand to seal the deal. "You want to go through everything here and then see my homes, or do you want to see the homes first?"

"Let's work here today, maybe tomorrow and then go to Dallas."

"Fine. I'll schedule the plane on Sunday for the flight to Dallas. Now we can enjoy the morning and each other's company while we have breakfast."

"Just keep it cool between us, Jared," she said lightly and he smiled in return. "One more thing. In Dallas, I'll stay at my home."

"But my house is in far north Dallas. After Dad died, I sold the family home," he explained. "I didn't want to live there."

"I can drive back and forth for the short time we're there."

He shook his head. "You'll waste about four hours per day and slow this down. Just stay at my place."

"Very well, but when we first get there, I want to stay with Dad so I can talk to him. He gets lonesome, and I want to see how he's doing."

"Sure. Come when you're ready to go to work."

After breakfast, Jared left on business in Austin, saying something had come up and he couldn't make it back until five, so he would see her for dinner. Relief filled her that he would not be beside her all through the day.

What was it that he had said? It would be a lot more exciting staying with him in Dallas? She scoffed. With Jared, more excitement was exactly what she *didn't* need.

Jared wanted to keep Allison happy. He wanted her to finish the job because the Tylers had one of the best companies in antiques appraisals and sales. Also, the chemistry was still there between them, and he wanted to make love to her again. And she was responsive enough that he thought it would happen. Sparks flew every time they were together.

As he worked through the day, anticipation built for the evening with Allison. She surely couldn't expect to hold him to their all-business arrangement during the evening. Seduction might send her packing before the job was over, but a few kisses should be harmless. Besides, kisses were something they both wanted.

When he arrived at the mansion after five, he didn't see Allison, and the door to her suite was closed, so he assumed she was dressing for their evening out.

Jared showered and dressed in charcoal slacks, a gray sport coat and left the neck of his white shirt open at the throat. By ten minutes to six, he was waiting in the library where he had told her that he would be. He was early, but he wanted every possible minute of the evening with her.

He heard the click of her heels and looked up, coming to his feet while his heart lurched in his chest.

Her sleeveless red dress clung in all the right places, some soft material that on her took his breath away. Her blond hair was caught up on both sides of her head to fall loosely in back. The red high-heeled sandals emphasized her shapely legs.

"You're stunning, Allison. I liked working with your dad, but I have to tell you, this is a perk of dealing with Tyler Antiques and Appraisals that kills your competition."

She smiled at him. "Somewhere in there I think is a compliment that I need to say 'thank you' for. If my brother even had an inkling—"

"We will totally forget your brother for tonight. Sloan never has known and doesn't need to know now," Jared said. "Tonight doesn't count in our business agreement to keep things professional. You're a big girl now, and you can make your own decisions," he said. "Shall we go?" he asked, linking her arm in his and catching a scent of her perfume, perhaps bergamot and jasmine. She was total temptation. The air all but crackled between them when they were together in a room. Inside that staid, business-like professional was still the flirty girl he had seduced. Hot, passionate, fascinating to him, she was a continual pull on his senses.

"For a few hours tonight I'm going to see to it that you forget your brother and all the others in your life. The only person who will be in your thoughts is me," he said, so sure he could do what he said.

"Sloan can take care of himself," she said as she walked beside Jared. "I'm worried about guarding my heart against

the daredevil playboy friend of my brother. I know your
past history too well."

"You weren't scared before."

"I was younger and not as wise. Besides, you were sort
of ready to run when you found out who I was. That made
you even more tempting."

"So you have an ornery streak," he said, remembering
that encounter.

"I just didn't want my brother running my life. Not then,
not now. But he doesn't interfere badly now. He has too
much going on in his own life to bother with mine. I'm
just looking out for me."

"You don't need to have a guard up with me."

"We shouldn't even be going out together, and you know
it."

"But we are, and we'll have fun, and I'll kiss you good-
night, and you'll want me to."

"Maybe you need a little more self-confidence," she
said, and he smiled at her.

"We'll see if I'm on target."

"You're not the only one with self-confidence," she said,
turning to face him as they stopped beside his car. She
tapped his chest with her finger. "You won't forget our
kiss, either," she said.

"That statement just changed how late we'll be out.
We'll be home earlier than I first planned," he said in a
husky voice as he opened the car door for her.

"Maybe," she said. "You might enjoy yourself dancing so much you won't even remember the conversation
we just had." She slid into the car and looked up at him.

"Not in the next hundred years would I forget it." He
fought an urge to kiss her now. She was tossing challenges
his way as much as she had that night when she had been

in college. He closed her door and walked around to get into the car.

She changed the conversation to talking about items she had looked at today and which rooms they would go through tomorrow. She was quick and efficient at her job, and she would be finished faster than he had expected, a prospect that mildly disappointed him. He hated to see her go, because he suspected there would be no going out with her once she returned to her own world.

She had already made it clear that she didn't want an affair. He was a longtime family friend of both her father and brother, so he had to back off and leave her alone. Tonight was one of those exceptions, but she was probably not as wild and reckless as she had been six years ago.

He tried to focus on what she was telling him about a lamp in the mansion, but all he could think about was their conversation and how much he wanted to kiss her.

Did she really care whether or not they kissed? Would she go beyond kisses?

He drove to a restaurant set back in a wooded expanse with ponds, fountains and lights in the tall pines. Myriad tiny crystal lights also covered the sprawling restaurant and surrounding redbud trees, giving it a festive air, while music was piped outside along the entryway. Jared handed his keys to a valet and took Allison's arm as they entered the restaurant, his fingers closing lightly, feeling her warmth and silky skin. The contact heightened his desire. Appetite for dinner fled. All he really wanted was to pull her into his embrace.

They were seated in a secluded alcove where the soft piano music was muted. Candlelight from the center of the table played over her, reflected in the depths of her indigo eyes. How long until she would be in his arms? Could they both resist seduction?

"Let's have a glass of wine before dinner. All right?"

"Certainly."

After a discussion over the wine list, Jared ordered a bottle of chardonnay. As they sipped their wine, Allison knew it would be difficult keeping her mind on business when she was out with Jared, but she called upon her complete self-control. At every turn she tried to keep the conversation on the items in his mansion and the possible home in which they'd fit.

At one point Jared set down his goblet of pale wine. "You have all this in your head, don't you? You remember everything."

"Maybe not everything, but a lot of it. I also have it saved on my iPad, so I don't have to solely rely on memory. I remember it because I love antiques, beautiful furniture and pieces that are also interesting. I hope to find people who really want the items you sell."

"I guess I understand that because I remember everything I've brought up in the salvage business. It's exciting to find a seventeenth- or eighteenth-century ship and bring back artifacts. They hold fascination for me."

"It's the same thing, Jared," she said. "You have to wonder about the people who owned them and what kind of lives they led."

He smiled at her. "You meant it when you said you love your job. That's good, because your customers will feel that enthusiasm. It makes me feel you'll do a great job for me, which, of course, I already know you will from working with your dad. But if this were my first time, I would feel in good hands."

"Jared, you're in really good hands."

She couldn't resist flirting with him for a moment.

Something flickered in the depths of his green eyes. He leaned over the table, closer to her, and his voice lowered. "Now, that's the Allison I know and want to love," he drawled.

"I think I started something I shouldn't have. I'm the one who wanted to keep things impersonal, but there is just something tempting about being with you—"

"That does it, Allison. Let's either dance or go home."

"Definitely dance," she said, smiling. "And I promise I will go right back to being ever-so-properly professional."

"Properly professional after the workday is over—there's a challenge if I ever heard one. Come on. We have a lot of dancing to catch up on."

"Regret we didn't dance later into the night before?"

"Not one regret of any sort about that night," he said in a warm tone that felt like a caress playing over her skin. He stood and held out his hand.

"None for me, either," she replied as she stood and placed her hand in his. His fingers curled around hers, and they walked to the small dance floor in the elegant restaurant.

They danced well together, and she liked being in his arms, smelling the fresh scent of his aftershave. The slow dance reminded her of the night they had spent together.

He spoke, and his breath was hot and tingly on her neck. "I still want you to watch me ride in the rodeo. I know you used to go when your brother competed."

She moved back and nodded. "Yes, I did, but I haven't seen one since college—over six years ago really," she said. "I like rodeos, except when someone I care about is riding. When Sloan rode, I was always afraid he would be hurt."

"You won't be worrying about me the way you did about Sloan, so it's time to see what fun a rodeo can be."

"You don't take no easily, do you?"

"Not if I want to hear a yes. I doubt if you do, either."

After two more dances they returned to their table just as the waiter brought tossed green salads for each of them.

Over lobster dinners, she studied him. As she set down her crystal glass of ice water, she said, "So tell me. There must be someone in your life for Sloan to tell me you're almost engaged. Who is the latest woman in your life? Is it still Dawn Rainsford?"

"No. That's over." His green eyes met hers in a steady gaze. "I am not engaged, getting engaged or planning to be engaged. That is your brother's whimsical wish and feeble effort to discourage you and to somehow get me to back off flirting with you or taking you out."

Allison smiled, amused by his description of Sloan's efforts to shelter her.

"And this guy in your life—Phillip—you're just good friends. That's your brother at work again. He's hell-bent on keeping us apart."

"Maybe he has sound reasons," she teased, making Jared's eyebrows rise. "Phillip and I are very compatible. He owns a hotel chain, and we met because he was interested in putting antique furniture in some of his penthouses and presidential suites."

"So no love affair with this guy?"

She shook her head. "No. We have the same interests, so we go to galleries, estate sales, the opera and concerts together, but there's nothing serious between us. He's company and someone to go out with, but that's all. He would say the same, although he does propose periodically. He says it would be convenient for both of us, and we could start a family. We are both getting older."

"Allison, aren't you twenty-four? That's not exactly long in the tooth."

Laughing, she shook her head. "I've told him no, but he's nice to offer."

"He's not the guy for you. You need someone who can match your passionate nature," Jared stated, giving her an intense look that ignited a heated response in her and made her forget dinner. "You need something more between you than the ballet and shared business interests."

She tore her gaze from Jared's. "Phillip and I have a good time. Sloan has my best interests at heart."

"I know he does, but you can take care of yourself. And he doesn't need to tell you that I'm engaged. You're very honest brother really loses it when it comes to watching over you."

She shrugged. "Sloan's just looking out for me."

"Enough about Sloan. Tell me about the jobs you've had. What is the oldest item you've dealt with, the biggest estate?"

Aware of Jared's constant gaze, she thought back. "The first question is more difficult to answer because I've dealt with so much that's old. The second is easy. Yours." While she talked, she was aware of his undivided attention.

Noticing Jared's appetite was as poor as hers, she wasn't surprised when he asked her to dance again, and she readily agreed.

Slow dancing to old favorites, dancing faster to some new ones, they reminisced about growing up for what seemed like hours. Finally he took her hand. "I think it's time we head home."

"Definitely," she said. His words played over her. He had made it sound as if they were going to their home, as if they were doing something ordinary that they did often.

Her heartbeat sped up, because she remembered their conversation about kisses tonight. Jared had not forgotten any more than she did. Could she say no to his seduction?

As he drove back to the mansion he had inherited, their conversation was still about general topics. She couldn't help but wonder about Jared and his wild life, the risky things he liked to do. She might be tempted to do something wild with him, but she couldn't get away from her years of caution.

In spite of their hot attraction, Jared wasn't the man for her. She didn't want a brief fling with him, because Jared could be a heartbreaker.

What was worse, he was pure temptation. She liked flirting with him, liked being with him, dancing with him. Even more, she liked his hot kisses. And he liked her business, understood it. It was the other side of his life that made a relationship with him impossible. That was all the more reason to do her job, stick to being professional and get through the mansion quickly, so she could go home and forget him.

"A penny for your thoughts," he said.

"You wouldn't want them even for free. There has been nothing professional about tonight. This is breaking my own rule."

"You have rules for your life?"

"Only where you're concerned," she replied with a tilt of her head. "There's something about your devil-may-care attitude that makes me toss caution aside, too. I need some rules to cover dealing with you."

"You know that's a challenge."

"I have no intention of flinging challenges at you."

"Tell me that you haven't enjoyed the evening."

"You know the answer to that one, so don't be smug about it."

"I wouldn't think of it."

"When you finish dealing with this mansion and the things inside, what will you do?" she asked.

"Go back to my regular life, running the family company, which is a full-time job and one I like."

"Then you understand how I feel about my work."

As he talked, they reached the gates of the mansion. With a wave to the gatekeeper, Jared drove to the rear of the house. Landscape lights illuminated the area, and Jared draped his arm across her shoulders as they walked inside.

They entered through the back hall into an entryway, and then he directed her to the kitchen.

"We can have a nightcap, cocoa, wine, coffee. What's your preference?"

"Just ice water," she answered, setting down her purse on the granite counter.

They sat in the living area adjoining the kitchen and talked, innocuous conversation about first one thing and then another, things she knew she wouldn't even remember in the morning. Underneath the conversation was a running current of awareness that they would kiss good-night.

Anticipation built until she stood and told him that she needed to call it a night. He followed her upstairs and stopped at the door of her suite.

"You know I had a great evening. Thank you for dinner," she said. When he placed his hands on her waist, her heartbeat quickened as she looked up into his eyes.

"I remember some words about kisses tonight. So at least I can kiss you good-night."

"Against all sensible judgment. We shouldn't, and we both know it," she whispered, though she wanted the opposite of her words.

"I know no such thing. Let me show you that you really don't, either." He slid his arm around her waist to draw her closer, then he bent down and paused, his gaze on her mouth.

She inhaled, trying to catch her breath. She expected his kiss, wanted it, her body thrumming with anticipation as her lips parted. "Jared," she whispered.

Then he edged closer to brush her lips with his.

The moment her mouth touched his, she closed her eyes. All she could hear was her drumming heartbeat. She wound her arm around his neck. At last...the kisses she had dreamed about, had tried to forget.

Kisses that were even better than she remembered.

# Four

She opened her eyes to look into his. In those depths of green, desire blazed, making her heart pound. While heat filled her, she went weak-kneed, clinging to him. The six years since their last kisses seemed to vanish.

She wanted him as if it were still that long-ago night when they had made passionate love for hours. She had wanted him then because he was the most exciting man she knew, the best looking, the most fun to flirt with. She hated to admit to herself that he still fit those descriptions. They had fire when they were together, an electrifying passion she had never found with anyone else.

As he leaned over her, his arm tightened around her, and he kissed her hard.

With a pounding heart, she kissed him back, holding him tightly. His hair, slightly coarser than hers, was sensuous as she ran one hand through his thick locks. Desire built to an extent she hadn't dreamed would happen. Couldn't happen. Not this time around. She was older, wiser. He was a man off-limits. A few kisses shouldn't shatter all her preconceived notions about how kisses could be kept under control.

Moaning softly, she struggled for self-control. Pleasure and desire tore at her resolve until she surrendered. Yielding to the moment, she poured herself into kissing him.

His hands roamed slowly down her back and over her bottom, then up again, each stroke heightening her breathless need. As his fingers slid beneath the open neck of her dress, she could not stop him. He filled his hand with her, caressing her, causing streaks of pleasure to radiate from the light brushes of his fingers.

From somewhere deep inside her brain, she heard the voice of reason cautioning her. If she let him go any further, she wouldn't be able to stop.

"Jared," she whispered and moved away in a last-ditch monumental effort for self-control. While her heart pounded, she gulped for breath. "I don't want to get more deeply involved. Not at this point in my life. Six years ago I was young, having fun and that was a fling at a party. I have a job to do now, and I want to stick to it."

"First of all, you're still young and you can still have fun. And you don't work at night, and the kisses we just shared have nothing to do with the job you're doing."

"Let's stick to business. I don't need an affair right now," she said, though she wanted more than anything to step back into his arms. His argument tugged at her. The look in his eyes seduced her. The past few minutes spread heat and need through her. "Your kisses are devastating."

"Damn, Allison," he whispered, frowning. "You're saying contradictory statements while every inch of you is conveying pure desire. You liked kissing me, and you want to make love," he said in a thick voice that heightened her conflict.

"You're right, but you have hired me to do a job that I intend to stick to with a narrow-minded purpose." She drew in a deep, steadying breath. "Good night. It's been a great evening. Thank you." She entered her suite, closing the door and half expecting him to stop her.

Memories of his body, his hands and mouth on her and

the ecstasy in their wake, tore at her. Hot, frustrated, she let out her breath and walked into the room.

She couldn't continue working with him during the day, going out with him at night and kissing passionately before they parted. If she did, there wouldn't be many nights until she was fully involved with him. And that was not going to happen.

She drifted around the suite, unable to settle down, knowing sleep might not come for hours. Memories taunted her while longing made her body hot and prickly. How could she say no to him—even one more time? She thought about the life he wanted, the wild pursuits he had. Emotionally, she did not want to deal with loving a man who constantly risked his life. A man who would not settle down and marry and raise a family. Jared was definitely not the man to love.

A cold shower did not help. Water splashed over her while she ached for his touch.

She tried working. Far into the night she sat there writing, trying to concentrate on her notes, cataloging and taking pictures of everything in her suite. It was almost dawn before she fell into a restless sleep.

When she went to the kitchen in the morning, the cook was preparing food for the day. Marline turned to smile at her. "Good morning," she said. "Orange juice is in the pitcher and coffee in the pot. Food is on the counter and on the table. Also, I can cook you some eggs."

"You go ahead with whatever you're doing, thank you," Allison told her politely. She was relieved the cook was present, and she would not be alone with Jared. "I'll get my breakfast, and there's plenty here already fixed."

"Mr. Jared said to tell you that he had some business that came up. He will see you this afternoon. I will be finished working at noon and away for the weekend. I have plenty prepared, so just help yourself to whatever you want."

"Thank you," Allison replied. "Does he usually let you off for the weekend?"

"Yes, he does. But just so you understand, I'm only here to cook while you're working here. I hadn't set foot in this place until the day before you came. I work in Dallas, with Edith, the housekeeper."

"You've both been helpful and nice. Thanks for what you've done."

"We came a day early to get the place ready so you both could stay here while you work."

Feeling relieved there would be a few hours she wouldn't have to cope with her attraction to Jared, Allison poured coffee and orange juice and toasted a slice of bread. She hurried through breakfast so she could get more work accomplished while he was away, glad she wouldn't have distractions.

By the afternoon she had finished four rooms, taking pictures, writing brief notes and relying on the snapshots to convey the inventory. She wasn't as thorough as usual, figuring she could complete the tasks when she was back in her office and away from all temptation with Jared.

She was so absorbed in the work she nearly jumped when she heard a voice drawl from the open doorway.

"Miss me?"

"Actually, I've managed without you," she said, turning, trying to keep things light even though her heart tripped when she saw Jared. He had already shed his suit jacket and tie and unbuttoned his white dress shirt at the neck. As he entered the room, he rolled up a cuff, and she couldn't stop watching him.

"Shucks, I was hoping you had missed me and couldn't

work without me," he said, grinning at her. Her racing heart beat faster as he continued approaching her, his green eyes holding her transfixed. "I've missed you every minute since we parted last night, and I've wanted to pick up where we left off," he drawled in a deep voice. "If not that, then at least kiss you hello," he added softly, stopping inches in front of her and placing his hands on her waist.

As if trying to come out of a daze, she shook her head. "I don't think so, Jared."

"No fun, Allison," he whispered, looking at her mouth and making her breath catch. Her lips parted, and she wanted to lean toward him, close her eyes and let him kiss her.

Instead she shook her head again and held up her notebook between them. "I've done nine rooms so far. We should walk through them so I can get your comments about the things in each."

He looked amused. "All right. We'll continue this discussion after dinner tonight."

"Jared—"

"You have to eat. We enjoy being together. This job won't last long, and it may be a lot longer than six years before we see each other again. Matter settled. I'll take you to dinner tonight. We can go two-steppin' at a fun honky-tonk."

"You are so incredibly sure of yourself."

"I know what I want, and I think I know what you want. Right?"

"Let's look at the rooms."

His smile widened as he nodded. Exasperated with him, she leaned closer and tapped his chest with her finger, looking into his green eyes.

"So if I stop fighting you, we'll have a full-blown affair?"

"Why do I think you want this as much as I do?" he asked, his smile vanishing as desire flared in the depths of his eyes.

"Not this time. I have responsibilities I didn't have before. And if did, you can kiss your friendship with Sloan goodbye. He's rather unforgiving sometimes."

"I don't think your brother has to know everything that you and I do."

"No, he doesn't, but he's already called." At Jared's look of surprise she added, "In good conscience I told him that you were at work. But don't worry, he'll keep up with both of us while this job in happening. You know I'm right."

Frowning, Jared stared at her. "Sloan is in Dallas, and we're far away in Houston. He has his own family now to worry over. You're no longer eighteen years old. Yet I shouldn't be surprised because he called me, too. I think he was overjoyed that I was at work."

"As a matter of fact, he's glad the job is going well. And he's extremely happy you're working on your own business matters."

"Does he do this all the time with you?"

"Not at all. You bring this on. He knows you too well."

"Thank goodness you don't take everything he says to heart."

"He hasn't realized I can make my own decisions. I'm not worried about Sloan, and I don't think you really are, either."

Jared's frown disappeared. "I still want to take you to dinner and dancing. And if they happen, kisses are harmless. Even your brother won't get worked up if he finds out we've kissed." He jumped in to stave off her argument. "Dinner is still on. Enjoying each other's company does not necessarily mean seduction."

"Jared, you and I cannot get personal on a small scale," she finally stated in exasperation.

He smiled and caressed her throat. "That's what keeps it so interesting," he said. "So how soon would you like to quit for the day?"

"I'm getting a lot done. I'd like to work until six." Trying once again, she warned, "Dinner is asking for trouble, and you know it."

"Not when you're circling the room doing the two-step, it won't be. Relax. Trust me, and I'll show you we can have fun together, enjoying each other's company."

Knowing she wasn't going to win this battle, she conceded. Getting back to work, she walked beside him and talked to him about the rooms she had done.

"I'll help you, unless you'd prefer working alone."

"You can help," she said, passing a notebook and pen to him. "I'll tell you what to write."

"Sure," he said. He stuck to business, which was a relief to her, and finally at six o'clock when the clock in the hall chimed, he held out her notebook. "Six it is. The witching hour. Time to get ready for our evening out."

"We could just keep working and really get things done."

"We could, but we're definitely not going to. C'mon, we'll get ready. You'll be glad you did. How much time do you want? Meet here at half past seven?"

"Fine," she said, picking up her things. He took them from her.

"I'll carry these until you get to your room."

"You know, I shouldn't have been surprised to hear from Sloan. Or that he called you, either. Actually, Sloan's actions don't worry me. He's too overprotective. Always has been. He didn't want me to have a driver's license until

I was eighteen. Thank heavens Dad prevailed. But I didn't drive without one of them in the car until I was seventeen."

Jared smiled. "You're good to put up so patiently with your brother. I have to say, the last fight we had, we were probably about nine years old. He gave me a bloody nose. Later he said he was sorry."

She smiled. "I don't think you'll have to fight Sloan. At least not about us getting involved."

No, she thought as she entered her room. The only fighting would be her fighting her attraction to Jared.

With eager anticipation, Jared waited in the library. He'd thought about Allison all day and he couldn't wait for her to appear. When had he ever been this anxious for a date? He dismissed his worries about Sloan. Allison didn't seem too concerned about what her brother thought, and Jared didn't see any chance of losing his long-time friend, unless he broke Allison's heart, which just plain wouldn't happen. She wasn't going to run any risk of falling in love. He thought he had allayed her fears about trying to buy their family business, something he definitely was not aggressively pursuing. Now if he could figure a way to calm her fears about his love of exciting, challenging endeavors, she would stop resisting him so strongly. The last was the stumbling block, because her family loss would never cease hurting, and she was so afraid of losing someone she loved again.

She came through the door and his heart thudded. His mouth went dry and he had to control an urge to cross the room, take her into his arms and kiss her.

"You look gorgeous," he said, unable to keep the huskiness out of his voice. He didn't say it, but she looked hot and sexy, too. His gaze drifted over the pale blue Western shirt that was unbuttoned far enough to give him a glimpse of tempting curves. The shirt was tucked into her tiny waist with a hand-tooled leather belt on jeans that were tight enough to send his temperature soaring.

He wasn't aware of crossing the room until only inches separated them.

"Lady, you look hot enough to melt a glacier."

"Thank you, I think," she answered. "You look pretty good yourself, cowboy."

Her hair fell loosely, framing her face, that yellow-blond hair that was a constant temptation to run his fingers through. He wanted to peel her out of her skintight clothes and make love to her. Instead he took a deep breath before winding her arm through his.

"Let's go," he said, looking down at her. Her scent was so enticing, eagerness bubbled up in him. He had waited all day to be with her, and finally she was with him for the evening. He picked up a broad-brimmed black Stetson and placed it on his head. In the hall she stepped away to get her own black Western hat. "Let's see what the evening brings," Jared said.

"Bushels of dancing," she replied. "I haven't done this in such a long time that I almost didn't pack these clothes."

"I'm glad you did. I'll try in every way to make the evening memorable," he said, slipping his arm around her waist and catching another whiff of the perfume she wore. His pulse was already doing its own crazy two-step.

He wanted to dance with her, flirt with her and come home and make love the rest of the night. She, on the other hand, wanted to stick to mere kisses, if that. What an impossible challenge, he thought.

At the car he held the door, and when she slid onto the seat, his gaze raked over her jeans that pulled tightly on her thighs. He inhaled, trying to steady his breath.

In minutes they were headed toward the highway and an evening that promised to be one of the best of his life.

At eleven o'clock they still circled the floor in a two-step. Allison could dance all night with him, and that was a better option than anything else she wanted to do with Jared. The sight of him melted her and made her heart race. Tall, lean, looking all cowboy and incredibly handsome, he was too sexy in his tight jeans and wide hand-tooled belt that rode low on his hips.

Could she stick by what she had told him? She reminded herself again to resist his charm. Get through the next few nights and this job would be over, she told herself, and she might not ever see him again.

He seemed willing to dance the night away, continuing without a word about going home. She hadn't danced like this in a long time—fast, constant, energetic. The more they danced, the more vitality and energy seemed to radiate from him. It was after midnight when she pointed out the time.

"Let's go home, Allison," he said, leaning close to her ear. "The band will be quitting soon anyway."

As soon as she nodded, Jared took her hand and they headed toward their table. Minutes later, they stepped into the cool night. Music and light spilled out with them, and Jared caught her, spinning her around on the wooden front porch of the sprawling honky-tonk.

She danced with him, their boot heels scraping the floorboards of the porch until he pulled her to him, and she laughed, bracing her hands against his chest.

"C'mon," he said, taking her hand.

She rushed down the steps to keep up with his long legs.

"Lady, that's the most fun I've had in a long time."

"I agree," she admitted, receiving a wide grin from him and knowing she shouldn't encourage him.

They talked all the way to the mansion, and inside agreed to have hot chocolate and some cookies. Vitality still oozed from him, and she sat and talked, aware the hour was growing really late but hating to end the evening.

Finally she stood, holding her empty mug. "Jared, the sun will be coming up soon. I need to get some sleep."

He came to his feet, picking up his mug and an empty plate. "All right, darlin'. Let's go to bed."

His words evoked the sizzling reaction she was certain he intended.

Ignoring him, she placed her mug in the kitchen sink. He draped his arm lightly across her shoulders as they climbed the stairs. At the door to her room, he turned her to face him, slipping his arm around her waist.

"Tonight was even greater than I expected. It's good to be with you, Allison."

"I had a wonderful time, too. I haven't been dancing like that since college. Thanks for the evening," she said, thinking how polite they each sounded. Yet as she stood there looking into his green eyes, desire was hot, palpable and tugging at her. When her gaze lowered to his mouth, her heartbeat quickened. In spite of all her reasons to avoid more sensual encounters with him, she wanted to kiss him.

Inhaling deeply, she glanced up to catch him looking at her mouth and then meeting her gaze. She couldn't wait for him to kiss her. As if she had no control over herself, she moved slightly closer to him, reaching up to place her hand on his shoulder.

"Allison." His whisper coaxed her closer, his husky tone enveloping her.

Her breath left her as she slipped her hand to his nape and watched him lean toward her. Wanting him more than ever, she closed her eyes. Reason shattered and desire burned while she stepped into his embrace. His arm tightened around her waist. His mouth opened hers, and his tongue played over her lips, before he kissed her deeply in a heart-stopping, breathtaking kiss.

He had to feel and hear her pounding heart. How could a kiss conjure up such magic as to melt her resistance? Wrapping both arms around his neck, she clung tightly, pressing against him even before his hand slipped over her bottom and then pulled her closer.

His hand caressed her throat and gradually slipped lower to unfasten the buttons of her shirt and allow him access. Finally, pushing away her lacy bra, he cupped her breast. His hands were warm, caressing her. Moaning with pleasure, she tugged at the buttons on his shirt and then ran her hand across his chest, tangling her fingers in his thick mat of chest hair.

His passionate kisses deepened while he walked her backward into her suite. Continuing to kiss her, he swept her into his arms to carry her to the bed.

Summoning willpower, she grasped his shoulders. "I can't, Jared," she whispered. "This isn't what I came to do," she said, wanting him more than she ever had.

He put her down on the bed. His green eyes had darkened with passion while his mouth was red from their kisses. Locks of black hair tumbled over his forehead. His unbuttoned shirt was open, revealing his muscled chest. Longing tore at her to pull him down to the bed, to kiss him senseless and make love for the rest of night.

He slowly straightened, standing in silence to look down at her. "I'll do what you want," he whispered. "But someday, you won't tell me no."

Her heart thudded. She wanted to toss caution, wisdom, everything aside and risk a broken heart, but she held back.

Fighting what she wanted with all her heart, she stared silently at him as he stepped away. His jeans bulged, and he looked like a man interrupted in the throes of making love.

"You know what you want," he whispered.

She fisted her hands to keep from reaching for him. For another long minute they stared at each other. Then he gave her a sweeping glance and left, closing the door behind him.

She sat up, clinging to the bed, telling herself not to run after him or call out to him. "Let him go," she whispered to herself. "Let him go." He would break her heart in every way. She couldn't deal with his lifestyle, and she couldn't have a casual affair. At this point in her life, she was ready for marriage. She wondered if he truly would ever be ready for a deep, lasting commitment. As for his lifestyle—his wild hobbies could be devastating. She wanted a quiet, ordinary life with a man who loved her. A man whose biggest risk was to drive on a vacation.

If only she didn't have this intense, hot reaction to Jared.

Still now her mouth tingled, and her body was on fire. Every nerve sizzled. She wanted his kisses and caresses even more because she already knew the ecstasy of his lovemaking. Why had she found this in Jared, someone so totally unsuitable for her?

Shaking her head, she slipped off the bed and went to shower, moving automatically with her thoughts on Jared and her body still vibrating from his touch. She had more than a week to go with him. Maybe weeks. Should she let go, take some risks herself?

An hour later she lay in darkness, still in torment, continuing to long for him while sleep eluded her. She glanced toward the door. "Are you sleeping, Jared?" she whispered.

Sunday they flew to Dallas and she took the day off, driving to her condo, which was near her family home.

Relieved to be away from Jared and temptation, she left later to spend the evening with her dad.

Early Monday, she'd received a text message from Jared telling her that he had gone to his office and would see her in the late afternoon. She followed his directions to his home, in a gated community of multimillion-dollar estates.

As soon as she gave the gatekeeper her name, large iron gates swung open. She followed the winding drive through an area thick with oaks until the road curved and only a few scattered ones remained in view. All her attention was drawn to the three-story Greek Revival mansion with wings, a wide porch across the front, a portico in the center entrance and tall, graceful Corinthian columns along the porch. The mansion was not what she had imagined Jared would own. She had envisioned something smaller, less breathtaking, less imposing that matched his laid-back personality. He had grown up in a home very much like her own, only a few blocks away from her family home. That was still what she had pictured him living in, not this magnificent mansion.

She parked in front, and the wide door opened. A tall sandy-haired man invited her inside. "Miss Tyler, I'm Stan Pinchly, Marline's husband. Please call me Stan. If you'll follow me, Jared has already left for his office."

"Thank you," she said, following him along a wide hallway that held a rectangular reflecting pool with a splashing fountain, marble floors, potted palms and oil paintings along the walls. A curving staircase led to the second floor, and she followed Stan into the living area of a suite of rooms.

"I'll bring your things up, and if you need anything, just let me know."

"Thank you, Stan," she replied, looking at sunlight spilling through wide windows, highlighting a fruitwood sofa upholstered in bright red poppies with two red wing-back chairs and a fruitwood rocker. Shelves of books lined one wall of the room, while art hung on the others. She walked through to the large bedroom, her gaze on an imposing four-poster bed that stopped her in her tracks. She couldn't help but picture herself in it with Jared, his arms wrapped around her, the sheets a tangled mass.

Trying to erase the torrid image, she shook her head. But it persisted.

Jared was even more appealing than he had been when she had been eighteen. And far more dangerous to her heart now. They were getting to know each other, and the more time they spent together, the more she wanted to be with him.

Tonight, would she be able to resist his kisses? Did she even want to? Despite his opinion, they could never be called harmless. Not at all. They were the beginnings of a powerful seduction.

# Five

Jared entered the restaurant and headed through the main lobby for the room reserved for their business breakfast club. He passed a splashing fountain and pots of ficus trees, his footsteps cushioned by the thick, deep blue carpet.

The club had two dozen members. Each one had achieved millionaire status or more, and Jared had known eight of them since high school or earlier, including Sloan, his closest friend.

Jared entered the private room where long, linen-covered tables formed a U shape in front of mahogany-paneled walls. Paintings of hunting scenes with hounds and men on horses hung on the walls, each picture in an oversize dark wood frame. Near the tables, members stood in clusters, some with morning drinks of orange juice or Bloody Marys in their hands.

Across the room, Sloan stood in a circle of men and waved, motioning Jared over. As Jared greeted other members and walked around the room toward his friend, he thought of Allison's silky blond hair. Sloan had no such inheritance. His straight light brown hair was combed neatly away from his face. He did not have Allison's indigo eyes, but a far lighter shade of blue. There was a faint facial resemblance in their bone structure, but no one would pick them out of the crowd as brother and sister.

Tall, broad shouldered, Sloan was a great friend, except where his sister was concerned. When it came to Allison, Sloan lost his calm balance and became far more the mother bear than a mother hen.

Wearing a pin-striped tailor-made suit, Sloan looked the successful businessman he was, but Jared still saw the gangly friend who was competitive in sports, ready for fun on the weekends and a class-A worrier, who throughout college always saw to it that they had a designated driver from parties and bars.

"I thought maybe you would be in Houston," Sloan said, shaking hands in greeting with Jared, looking intently at his friend.

"No, I'm right here at home. Your sister is taking inventory, and she said your dad will do the research. She sends the info and pictures back to him on her laptop." He had no plan to let Sloan in on the secret that Allison was in Dallas.

"She's been a tremendous help to him, and she enables him to keep the business, which is good. We're all happy about that. I figured you'd go rushing down there to see what she's doing."

"I hired her to deal with the house." He clapped his friend on the shoulder. "So how are the little Tylers?" Jared asked, knowing Sloan would stop thinking about Allison if the subject of his children came up.

"Virginia and Megan still treat Jake like their doll. He loves the attention, so they're all happy. I expect this to last until he's old enough to get into their things." Sloan pulled out his phone and touched it, holding it for Jared to look. "This picture was taken last night."

Jared looked at Sloan's wife, Leah, her mop of curly brown hair framing her face. She held all three children, with the baby in the middle and both little girls on each side. Virginia had Leah's thick curls while Megan had silky blond hair and big eyes, making Jared think of Allison.

"Good-looking family, Sloan. That's great."

"It's super great," he said, putting away the phone. "Having a five-year-old, a three-year-old and a one-year-old keeps Leah hopping."

"Keeps you busy, too."

He nodded. "But never too busy." He leaned in toward Jared and said in a conspiratorial tone, "I've got some property that will go on the market in a few months that's right by your office. You might want to look at it sometime."

"Sure, I do. Where is it—the old building to the north?" Jared asked, thankful they had moved on to other topics.

"Here come the Delaneys," Sloan said, giving a slight wave, and Jared turned to see Will, Zach, Ryan and his brother-in-law, Garrett Cantrell, with them. They were all tall men. Zach bore little resemblance to his brothers that Jared could see with his curly brown hair and blue eyes. It still was difficult to believe the demolition man had stopped traveling to jobs all over the world and settled into married life without a grumble.

As they greeted each other, Sloan smiled. "It's good to see all of you. Seems like at least one of you has missed the past few breakfasts. How's the family, Will? How's little Caroline and the baby?"

"They're great. Ava said Caroline is a big help to her, so that's good. Caroline loves little Adam."

"It's nice you named your baby for your older brother, Caroline's daddy," Jared said. "You've been a super uncle to her after Adam's death, and now you're really a dad to her. You're doing a great job."

"Thanks, Jared. Caroline loves having her little brother named for Adam. To her, he's not a half brother, he's just her brother. All of us like having another Adam in the family."

"That's great. We'll have to get together," Jared said. "I haven't seen the Delaney families for a while. We'll have a shindig soon." He glanced around. "It looks as if the breakfast buffet is set up. Everyone ready?"

As they joined the line that was forming, Jared fell into step beside Ryan. "We'll leave the old married men to themselves. At the moment they're looking at kid pictures." Ryan grabbed a plate and began piling on food.

"Ryan, I've been to Houston. The house is filled with such beautiful old things that I—"

"Jared, don't even ask again. None of us want anything," Ryan said, shaking his head and smiling. "Do what you want with your inheritance."

"All right. Soon you won't even have a choice."

"Suits me fine." He added more to his plate. "In August I'm riding in a rodeo in Tombstone. Any chance you'll be participating, too?"

"That rodeo is not on my calendar, so maybe you'll win one this year."

Ryan grinned. "Now if I can just find a third one, I'll have a banner year with my winnings."

"That's a positive outlook," Jared teased as Ryan again turned his attention to the food spread before them.

Jared thought he might get through breakfast and away without Sloan mentioning his sister again, but as they left the restaurant, Sloan turned to him. "Hey, buddy, sorry I bugged you about Allison."

Jared laughed as he shook his head. "No, you're not sorry. If I left here for Houston, you'd call me tonight and start quizzing me."

Sloan shrugged. "Maybe so. I just have to take care of

my family. She's an innocent, and you're a wild man who
would break her heart in every way."

"As I recall, your sister's over twenty-one, and I suspect
she can take care of herself plenty well."

"Allison is a worrier just like I am."

"What's this? Worry runs in the family? Worry is not
an inherited trait, my friend."

"The propensity to worry may be inherited." He reached
out to shake hands with his friend. "It was good to see
you, Jared."

"You too, though I feel sorry for Virginia and Megan
when they start dating. What a dad you'll be for your girls
to bring some boy home to."

Sloan smiled. "Maybe I'll mellow out by then."

"You'll be worse. I'll call you about that property."

"Okay. See you," Sloan said as Jared walked away to
his car. He felt no guilt for not telling Sloan that Allison
was also in Dallas. Sloan would find out soon enough, and
besides, it would save him from worrying.

His thoughts shifted to Allison and his step quickened.
He was going to the office for a couple of appointments,
but he wanted to get through with them and get home as
soon as he could. He wanted to be with her, and he already missed her as if they had been separated days instead of overnight.

Throughout the morning, Allison prowled the first floor
of his mansion. Marline cooked, but had already told Allison that she and Stan would leave at noon. Jared had said
he would have to be gone until late afternoon, which suited
her. For the afternoon she would be alone and probably
could work faster. Later, she would be alone with Jared, a
prospect that made her tingle.

His home was beautiful. She far preferred it to his inherited mansion. There was more light, more windows, giving the house an airier feel. The antiques he had took her breath away. Apparently they had the same taste, and Jared had acquired some fantastic furniture and pieces.

At two o'clock she was in the study when she heard the bell at the front door. If Jared had expected someone, he would have told her. She assumed it was a delivery that had been approved to get past the gatekeeper.

On her way to the door, she glanced out a window and saw a long black limo at the curb, and her curiosity grew. Was Jared out there with a limo?

When she opened the door, she looked into the light brown eyes of the most beautiful auburn-haired woman she had ever seen. Tall, with a full figure, she wore a clingy white suit. Allison knew instantly she was facing Dawn Rainsford, whose eyes narrowed as she stared at Allison.

"Are you living here?" she asked in the same throaty voice Allison had heard in her movies.

"Yes, I am," Allison replied, startled and biting back the introduction she had started to make. Silence stretched between them.

"Is Jared home?"

"He's at the office." Dawn eyed her from head to toe, looking with haughty disdain on her T-shirt, jeans and jogging shoes. When her eyes met Allison's gaze again, Allison noted her lashes were thick, too long to be real, but beautiful.

"You might as well pack your things, whoever you are. I think you'll be moving soon," she said finally.

Allison regained her composure. "I'm Allison Tyler," she said.

"I'm sure you know who I am."

"I'm sorry. Your name is…" Allison couldn't resist,

and then felt guilty for the brief ornery streak that motivated her.

"It's Dawn. Dawn Rainsford." She turned and headed back to the limo. "Tell Jared I was here," she ordered over her shoulder. A chauffeur stepped out to open the door for her.

When the limo pulled away, Allison shut the door and leaned against it, surprised and disappointed. Evidently Dawn Rainsford was not as out of Jared's life as he had indicated. Allison could not imagine she was out at all if she wanted to be in his life. Dawn Rainsford looked as if she could have whatever and whomever she wanted.

Struggling to put Jared out of mind, Allison returned to her work. Hoping to get as much done as possible and finish her task, she strolled through his home and made notes as she went. By half past three she was satisfied she had done as much as she could until she went over the place with him, which apparently wasn't going to happen today. She really didn't care to see him right now anyway.

As planned earlier, she left to drive to her dad's for dinner. Before leaving Jared's home, she wrote a note and placed it on the kitchen table.

It was well over an hour's drive even in four o'clock traffic to her father's house. She entered through the back door, calling out to him, relieved to escape Jared's house and talking to him about Dawn.

Tempting smells of roast beef and hot bread greeted her, eliciting a smile. "Dad, I'm here," she called.

Herman Tyler appeared, a smile causing his wide blue eyes to crinkle at the corners as he held out his arms. She walked into his embrace, catching scents of garlic and onions. "It smells wonderful in here."

"I made a pot of stew. Come in and tell me about the mansion. You're doing a good job, and you've been correct in your descriptions and notes so far." He stirred the stew, the delicious smell wafting out from the open lid.

"Thanks, Dad."

"There are some pieces that are very old and very valuable. Others are just so beautiful, it wouldn't matter if they weren't old and rare. How will some of the things look in his Dallas home? That's a first for you."

"Yes, it is. I made it clear to him that all I can do is give him my opinion."

"Well, he knows where you grew up."

"That's what he said," she remarked.

"Let's go sit in the family room. Would you like a glass of wine with me?"

"Sure, Dad. You sit, and I'll get it. Your usual cabernet sauvignon?"

"Yep. Haven't changed."

She smiled as she got the bottle from the counter. "Mind if I open a white?"

"Of course not. It's good to have you home."

In minutes they sat in the family room. She rocked in her favorite rocking chair while her dad talked about the family. "As always, Sloan calls every day to see how I feel. He called about four o'clock today. He always asks how the job is going, and I told him about Jared asking you to see what would fit in his Dallas and Wyoming homes. Your brother was surprised you're in town. He said he may drop by on his way home from work."

"He's usually in a rush to get to his own home," she said, though she was absolutely certain her brother would appear within the hour. He wouldn't miss a chance to grill her about Jared.

"Sloan is probably scared now that Jared will ask you out."

"That doesn't worry you, does it, Dad?"

"Of course not. I like Jared. I know you were a little angry he left the offer open to buy our business, but he's a businessman. Actually, it's nice, because if we should have to sell, or decide we want to sell, I would prefer to sell to him. He'll take care of the business. As far as your brother is concerned, I know you long ago learned to pay no attention to his worrying over you."

"Well, it isn't the end of the world if I go out with Jared, but Sloan should stop worrying about it."

"That's like telling the sun to stop coming up in the morning," her father replied, chuckling. "Nothing can keep Sloan from worrying about us. If he isn't worrying about me, he's worrying about you."

Nodding, she said, "Enough about Sloan. Let's talk about Jared's mansion. This is a good job for us, Dad."

"Yes, it is. We should have a beautiful catalog of Jared's things, unless he decides to keep most of them."

The sound of the back door closing halted their conversation.

"Hey, there," Sloan called, sweeping into the room.

She greeted him, and her dad asked if Sloan wanted to join them in a glass of wine.

"Thanks, no. Can't stay long," he said, perching on the edge of a chair and turning to her. "I didn't know you were back in Dallas. Jared didn't say anything about it this morning at breakfast club."

"Jared doesn't always mention things," she said, thinking about Dawn.

"Not if he doesn't want me to know about it," Sloan replied, still studying her.

"How's the family, Sloan? I haven't seen the little ones for over three weeks."

"When this job's over, you can keep all three of them some evening. That ought to be enough for you," he said.

"I'd love for them to come and stay all night. We'll have fun."

"That's a deal. You're a good aunt, sis. And the girls would love to come. The baby is too little to know what he's doing. I'll tell the girls, because it'll give them something to look forward to."

"Come by and bring the kids to see me first on your way to Allison's," Herman said and Sloan nodded.

"Did Jared hang out at his house today?" he asked Allison.

"I haven't seen Jared today at all," she said. Then she added, "I'll probably return to Houston tomorrow."

"Is Jared going to Houston?"

"You'll have to ask him, Sloan. I don't know what he's doing. I haven't talked to him. I'll tell you who I did see. Dawn Rainsford came by in her limo looking for Jared," she said, knowing that would please Sloan.

"What does she look like in person?" Sloan asked, sounding awestruck.

"She looked just like she does in her movies or on television or in ads. She's gorgeous."

"Jared does attract the ladies," Sloan said. "Dawn Rainsford… Did she come in?"

"We didn't exactly have tea together," Allison remarked. "You can save your questions for Sloan. I only had a brief encounter."

Sloan studied her, and she gazed back, sipping her wine. He stared at her. "So how's the job?"

"Very good. Ask Dad. Your friend has a great inheritance. That mansion is filled with beautiful antiques."

"I'm surprised Jared wants to sell the place and almost everything in it."

"If you could see the mansion, you'd know why," Allison said. "It's sort of gloomy."

"Well, I'd better hit the road because it's going to be a long commute home in this traffic." He turned to his sister. "Walk me to the door?"

She followed him to the back door, where Sloan turned to face her. "Don't go out with Jared," he said immediately in a hushed tone. "It doesn't sound as if there's much danger of that happening, but I'm warning you. He has a trail of broken hearts behind him, Allison. He isn't ready to settle down."

"I know," she said, studying her brother. "To tell you the truth, I'll be glad to be almost finished." She looked over her shoulder toward the family room. "I just don't want to worry Dad about it."

"Frankly, that's good news."

To hurry her brother along, she embraced him. "Tell the family hi and give them a hug and kiss for me," she said.

"That I'll do. See you," Sloan said, leaving. At his car he paused and waved. She watched him drive around the corner before closing and locking the door. Her cell phone chimed, and she took it out of her pocket to see it was a call from Jared. She placed it on a shelf by the back door and started to leave it when it rang again. She glanced at it once more and saw a familiar number. Picking up the phone, she answered to hear her friend Phillip, who asked her to dinner.

After, she rejoined her dad. "Phillip just called and asked me to dinner. I knew you wouldn't mind, so I told him to come join us. He'll be here shortly."

"Good," Herman said. "I'll check on the stew."

"While you do that, I'll set another place at the table," she stated, heading to the large kitchen with her dad.

Thirty minutes later she heard the door chimes and opened the front door to face a tall, broad-shouldered man

with blond hair and blue eyes. His smile revealed flawless white teeth.

"Come in. Dad and I are in the family room."

"How's the Houston job going?" Phillip asked, walking beside her.

"Very well. I'll be through and home soon."

"Good. Did you find lots of interesting items?"

"Yes. I can show you some pictures. Dad, here's Phillip."

The two greeted each other and soon they were sipping
wine and talking. As the men discussed the recent estate
sale they had both attended, she studied Phillip. He'd be
considered a handsome man by any female. Why didn't
she have the same electrifying reaction to Phillip she did to
Jared? She was far more compatible with Phillip. He was
interesting, handsome, successful—all descriptions that
would fit Jared—but there was no heart-stopping, breathless reaction when they touched or kissed. Phillip was nice,
pleasant, but she felt nothing toward him except friendship. She reminded herself that he was the type of man
she wanted to marry—reliable, safe, responsible. A man
who didn't want to take wild risks and enjoy adventures
that could be life threatening and—

"Allison?"

She realized both men were staring at her, and her dad
repeated her name.

"Sorry. I was thinking about some notes I made today
and wondering what I did with them. I didn't hear what
you said."

"I asked you to take Phillip to my office and pull up the
pictures you sent. He may be interested in buying something when that collection goes on the market."

"Sure," she said, standing at the same time as Phillip.
In minutes he sat at her father's desk, and she had pulled

a chair beside him while Phillip scrolled through the pictures on the laptop. She lost herself in describing the pieces as Phillip read her father's notes.

Herman stepped to the door. "Dinner's ready. You two come eat, and then you can come back and finish looking. Did you find anything, Phillip?"

"Yes, sir. There is a seventeenth-century German clock I'd like, especially if Jared agrees to sell it for the price you've placed on it."

"I think he'll accept whatever Dad suggests," Allison said, walking beside Phillip to the kitchen, where steaming bowls of stew awaited on the table. A platter with hot golden corn bread was in the center of the table.

Allison only half listened to the conversation through dinner while they talked about the antiques from the Delaney collection. She heard her phone ring once, and Phillip paused. "I think I hear a phone. It's not mine."

"It's mine," she answered. She flapped her hand, as if to dismiss it. "It isn't important. Sloan would call Dad's line."

Phillip looked at her with curiosity and then turned to continue his conversation with her dad.

By nine o'clock Phillip said he had to leave, and she followed him to the door.

"When will you be back in Dallas to stay?" he asked.

"Probably not for two more weeks," she answered. "I'll try to make it sooner."

"Call and let me know. There's a play coming up that should be good. It was successful on Broadway, and this is its first time in Dallas. It will be here early April."

"Great. I'll let you know as soon as I do when I'll be home."

"Thanks again for dinner."

"That was Dad's doing. Glad to see you," she said.

"It's good to see you. 'Night, Allison," he said and brushed a light kiss on her cheek.

She watched him get into his car and waved at him before he drove away. Closing and locking the door, she remembered Jared's kisses that ignited desire until it was a raging blaze. Why couldn't she feel that with a man like Phillip, the kind of man she intended to marry? She was sure there were women who would love to go out with him, and found him exciting and fun.

Of all men, why was she attracted to Jared?

When she rejoined her dad in the kitchen, he waved his hand. "Why don't you spend the night here? You can go to Jared's in the morning."

Smiling at him, she sat beside him. "I'll do that," she said, knowing it would please her dad, who no doubt was lonesome.

She didn't acknowledge her other reason for staying: she wouldn't have to see Jared tonight.

Not seeing him didn't mean, however, not thinking about him. She spent a restless night in her old bedroom, plagued by images of him in Dawn's arms.

In the morning she took her time leaving her father's house, in hopes that Jared would have already left for his office. She waited until almost nine o'clock to kiss her dad farewell.

She drove to Jared's house. To her surprise, his black low-slung sports car was in the rear driveway. She hoped Marline and others on his staff were present. She didn't care to deal with Jared right now. She didn't want to hear him tell her Dawn was definitely out of his life. Dawn had not gotten the message. Allison didn't want to think about his kisses, either.

She knew she had to interact with him at some point in

order to return to Houston and finish her task. But later was better than sooner in this case.

Steeling herself with a deep breath, she went to the back door and knocked. In seconds the door swung open, and she faced Jared....

And, like a billowing curtain, her resolve went out the window.

# Six

"Good morning. I'm glad you're back." Jared smiled, and she felt warmth settle on every inch of her, like honey oozing on bread.

All the coolness she'd mustered toward him dissipated in one single heartbeat. She drew a deep breath, passing him while he held the door, and caught a whiff of his masculine aftershave. He wore a tan Western shirt, jeans and boots.

Closing the door, he caught up with her, his fingers closing lightly on her arm as he turned her to face him. "I called you last night, and I sent you text messages."

"We had company when I visited with my dad. I stayed at his house all night." She forced herself to step out of his grasp. "Dawn came by here yesterday," she said, aiming for light and casual and missing the mark. She compounded it by gazing into his eyes. His sinfully appealing green eyes. "I—I think she left afterward for your office."

"She did. Allison, it is over between us. She was probably bored and couldn't think what else to do while she's in Dallas. She'll be in a show here that'll run for about two weeks. She means nothing to me. I seriously doubt if I mean anything to her."

"It doesn't matter, Jared. It was just a reminder that you

and I have different values, different lives," she said, feeling only a degree better.

"I don't think we have such glaring differences. Dawn shouldn't make any ripples between us, because she's out of my life."

"She hasn't gotten that message, Jared."

"She knows it full well, but if I talk to her again, I'll remind her." He closed the space between them and took her arm again. "In the meantime, let's forget Dawn."

"Consider it done." Regardless, she had to get out of this house. Get away from Jared as soon as possible. "How soon do we leave for Houston? I'd like to get back to work."

He stood looking at her, and she wondered what he was thinking. In spite of her determination to keep him at arm's length, right now her heart beat faster, and she was intensely aware of his hand lightly on her arm, his steady gaze holding hers.

"I'll talk to the pilot." Jared walked away. He pulled his cell phone from his pocket to confer with him. "We take off in less than an hour," he told her a moment later. "We can leave now for the airport."

"Fine. I'm ready to go."

It took her no time at all to grab her things, and within minutes, they were on their way. The ride to the airport was quiet. It wasn't until they were airborne that they started to talk. Jared shifted in his seat to look at her and asked, "How's your dad?"

"He's fine. He told Sloan that I was in Dallas. Sloan came by after work to see us. He stops by a lot to check on Dad."

"Sloan called me. Again. I saw him at breakfast club yesterday morning, and I didn't tell him you were working in Dallas. He thought you were still in Houston. He was less than happy with me for not mentioning it. I think

I made it clear to him that there is nothing between us, and this job will be over very soon. I told him that you're busy, and we haven't seen each other much."

Allison merely nodded.

"What did your dad think about the items in the mansion?"

"He's extremely pleased," she replied, relieved to get back to business. "He thinks you've inherited beautiful and valuable antiques, and we'll be able to have a successful sale."

"Good to hear."

"Dad has a partial draft of the catalog done with the pieces I've already inventoried." She pulled it out of her briefcase, and Jared moved closer to look, holding one side of the brochure when she opened it. They carefully went through it, commenting on the pictures and the descriptions.

"This is excellent, Allison," he said, and she looked up at him. Only inches separated them. He focused on her, and as she gazed into his clear green eyes that had always fascinated her, she forgot the business at hand. Her heartbeat quickened and she fought the urge to look at his mouth. Wanting to lean closer, she knotted her fists and tried to look away, to escape the mesmerizing draw of this potent man.

"I don't want to do this," she whispered, still frozen in his gaze.

"Yes, you do. As much as I do," he said softly, drawing closer. She couldn't get her breath. She wanted to reach for him, to wrap her arms around his neck and hold him while she kissed him, and he kissed her back.

When his gaze shifted to her mouth, her lips tingled. His head lowered before his lips brushed hers in a feathery touch that she should have barely felt. Her toes curled, her breath escaped her and her resistance crumbled. She closed her eyes while his mouth covered hers and his tongue slipped over hers.

As she shuddered, he caressed her nape. She wasn't capable of stopping him. She kissed him back with fervor. She knew one kiss would never be enough.

She couldn't get her breath when she finally pulled back. "I don't want to feel this with you," she said, as much to herself as to him. "We're not right for each other."

"I think we're as right as can be. Stop fighting it. Can't you feel it, Allison? Everything in you responds to me just as I respond to you. Darlin', we've got something special between us. You can't deny it," he whispered, staring intently at her.

She couldn't. She wanted to deny it, to fling the words in his face, but in all honesty, she couldn't say them, because they both knew there was no way to deny the attraction.

"You spin magic between us, weaving a spell around me," she said. "I need to finish this job and go home, before I'm hopelessly ensnared and in love, something you won't be."

"You'll never be 'hopelessly ensnared,'" he said. "You're far too independent. Besides, we're not even having an affair." He reclined back in his seat and stretched out his long legs.

"And we'll keep it that way," she added.

To her relief, when they reached the Houston mansion and she went directly to work, Jared remained remote, professional and totally focused on the task until half past five in the afternoon. Even so, she could not keep from noticing the flex of muscles in his arms if he lifted any of the furniture. His cotton sleeves were rolled up. When he knelt to look under furniture, his jeans pulled taut, molding to his muscled thighs. Everything he did drew her attention. Even though he might go half an hour without saying a word, having him beside her constantly was almost as much torment as when they flirted.

Finally he set the iPad on a table and placed his hand lightly on her arm.

"We should stop now for dinner. No working day and night. We've gotten a lot done today."

"But I want to get this job done," she said, facing him, looking into his searching gaze.

"Are you in a hurry now because of Dawn?"

"No. I believe what you said." She set down her pencil and paper and focused on him. "Jared, we have to face the facts. You're not the marrying kind, and I am. We're just not right for each other. All this going out at night, flirting, dancing, kissing—that all leads one direction, to an affair." When he was about to object, she stilled him with a hand. "You have a well-stocked kitchen. Let's eat here." The cook hadn't returned with them to Houston, but Allison figured they could find something to prepare. "I'll keep working. You can do what you want."

"We'll eat here, and I'll work with you," he said. "You can pause for a drink, can't you?"

His capitulation to her wishes made her happy, and she smiled at him. "Yes, I can. I'm quite ready for a break."

He touched the corner of her mouth lightly with his finger—a feathery touch that melted another bit of her resistance. "There—it's good to see you smile. C'mon. It's a pretty spring day. We can sit outside and have a drink. We can even go for a swim if you want. It is a heated pool."

"No, thanks, Mr. Tough Man," she said quickly as she joined him, and they headed down the hall toward the kitchen. "It may be a heated pool and a sunny day, but it's way too cool for me to swim. And it isn't officially spring yet, by the way."

"I'll keep you warm," he offered.

She laughed. "I'm sure you would. Thanks, but as enticing as your offer is, I'll pass. I do not swim before the traditional Memorial Day weekend at the earliest. In cooler climes, I do not swim until the Fourth of July. I'm not trying to live life on the edge or prove anything. You can meet life's challenges, but not me, thank you."

"I'm dealing with one of life's biggest challenges right now," he said, holding the back door for her and following her outside to the patio. He motioned in the direction of the outdoor kitchen and bar. "I'm trying to figure out how to get you to knock off working tonight, as well as a few bigger challenges you've thrown my way today."

"I definitely am not trying to challenge you," she said. "Far from it. Just ignore me and go on with your life."

"That, Allison, is a complete turnaround from the night we met. And I'm not accustomed to getting that reaction from a woman, particularly one I really like."

His words were heat and enticement. She fought her attraction to him, the constant pull on her to relax, flirt and do what he wanted.

"Before you know it, I'll be gone out of your life."

"The more you tell me things like that, the more I want to get past the wall you're throwing up between us. I know the warm, passionate woman behind the barrier."

"Jared, that's exactly what I'm struggling to avoid."

"Sit while I get us some light snacks and pour drinks. What will you have?"

She sat at the bar. "I'd prefer a margarita."

He became busy behind the bar and in minutes placed a bowl of roasted almonds in front of her, along with another bowl of green olives and a platter of chips and fresh salsa.

"I'll take this to the table," she said as he put them on a green tray. She set them on a nearby table, and he joined her to hand her a margarita with a salty rim and a lime slice.

Pulling his chair away from the table, he sat facing her, his long legs stretched out alongside her chair. He held up his glass. "Here's to a successful sale."

"To a very successful sale," she said, raising her glass to touch his lightly. He watched her intently as he sipped.

"To the most beautiful antiques dealer in the U.S.A."

She smiled and raised her glass again. "Whoever she is."

"You know exactly."

"Thank you, but you exaggerate. Besides, you can't have seen them all. You don't know who's out there."

"No, but I know who's here beside me," he said, leaning forward so he was close to her. His gaze roamed over her features, and she could barely get her breath.

"Don't make me regret coming out here," she whispered, thinking she should move, talk, do something or in seconds they would kiss.

"I miss the flirty college girl I knew six years ago."

"She's gone forever, Jared," she replied. "You can't get back time. It marches forward. In a blink of an eye, I'll be home and this job will be finished." She sat back and crossed her legs. "I made arrangements with Sloan that he'll bring his children over to stay the night with me when I get back. They are really adorable. I suppose that's one reason I've starting thinking about marriage so much," she said, changing their topic of conversation. She hoped to cool Jared's flirting and attention, and homed in on the best way she could think to do so. "They're such fun, even the baby, who is twelve months and not walking yet but crawling everywhere."

Jared sipped his drink and looked mildly amused, as if

he had figured out her purpose in talking about her nieces and nephew.

"Don't you love little kids, Jared?"

"I'm not around them. But I've looked at pictures of Sloan's kids, and they're cute."

"Sloan is the happiest he has ever been. That's another reason marriage appeals to me. I used to think my brother would never get married. Now that he did, he is so in love and so happy with his family."

"It's a trade-off. He gives up certain things and gains certain things."

"True, but what he gained is for a lifetime and too good to measure. What he gave up is fleeting and easily forgotten."

Jared nodded. "Well, the real trick is to find that absolutely one right person. But you're still tied down in a lot of ways."

"Tied down to love," she said, exasperated with his view of life and his determination to give up love and family for a few thrills and big risks. He sipped his cold beer and gazed beyond her, and her exasperation grew with his attitude.

There was only one way she could think of to prove her point to him.

Clamping her jaw closed, she got up swiftly and stepped over him so she sat astride him. At the same time she yanked off her shirt, pulling it over her head and dropping it. At once, his eyes widened and he looked startled.

Leaning forward, she kissed him on the mouth—a deep, passionate kiss.

His brief shock vanished as he embraced her and kissed her in return. She ran her fingers through his thick hair and along his nape while she leaned away to slip her other hand beneath his shirt and caress his chest.

He was warm, rock hard with muscles.

He filled his hands with her breasts, unfastening and pushing away her bra. Desire pooled within her, hot, spreading. Her hand slid down over his rough jeans, over his arousal that pressed tightly against the denim.

As abruptly as she had moved over him, she stopped and moved away, gasping for breath and stepping off his lap. Yanking her shirt back over her head, she sat again in her chair, turning it slightly to face him.

"That's the physical part of a good marriage," she explained. "Sex when you want it, hot, built on a bedrock of love, getting better with time, I'm sure. That's only one facet. How does that compare with climbing an icy glacier and coming home alone?" she asked. "You take your life and your preferences, and I'll keep mine, but they really don't mix."

He turned his chair closer with his legs touching hers and reached out to slide his arm around her waist. She wriggled back and smiled. "That was just to prove a point. No more kisses," she said, trying to ignore her pounding heart and control the longing to go back into his embrace.

He inhaled deeply, and she wondered whether she had started something she would regret. If he set his mind on seduction, she wasn't certain how long she could hold out.

Picking up her drink, she raised her glass. "Here's to happy adventures for you and a solid marriage for me."

His green eyes looked filled with speculation. He raised his bottle. "Solid? That's what you want? Not a love-filled marriage?"

"A love-filled marriage is solid," she replied before taking a sip. Frankly, she needed a moment to gather herself. His kiss had left her breathless, aching for more.

He moved closer. "You may have just started fires that can't be extinguished easily."

"I was just proving a point with you. Or at least giving you my view of marriage and family versus your lifestyle. To each his own."

He smiled, studying her, and she wondered what ran through his thoughts. "You'll miss a lot, Allison. And you weren't so ready to settle down when I met you."

"Of course not. I was in college and six years younger. Life changes a person. Now my dad isn't well, and the clock is ticking. I don't think I'll miss anything. Actually, I feel you're the one missing out on life."

"So we're at an impasse on our views of each other. When we kiss, though, the differences never seem to matter. You can't deny that. That missing out on love and family is a siren song that has ensnared many a man who never got to fulfill his dreams."

"You pursue your dreams, Jared, and I'll pursue mine. May we both find happiness." She stood up abruptly. "Now let's get back to business. My father is making arrangements to move the pieces from here to a Dallas auction site. He's aiming for early June. Before that he will have a presale where select buyers have first chance at the inventory. Phillip has selected three pieces that he'd like to buy, and I have my eye on buying a couple of things then, if you don't take them now. Don't ask which ones, because I want you to choose whatever you like."

"If you'd tell me now, you might ensure getting them," he said, looking more intently at her.

She shook her head. "No. You and I have the same tastes in furniture and decor. I wouldn't think of taking something you really like and want."

"Your choice. Just remember my offer. Speaking of offers—how about dinner?"

Before she could answer, his cell rang. He held it up to take the call, then stood and walked away from her to talk. She turned her attention to the view, enjoying the day, thinking about all he had said, remembering his kisses. He was gone longer than she had expected, and when he returned she watched him sit next to her again.

"Sorry. I may have to get back to Dallas on business soon. I think it would be best to go on to Wyoming tomorrow if you want."

"That's fine," she replied.

"I'll make the arrangements. It'll be cooler there. If you need a coat, because I'm sure you didn't bring one to Houston, we can get one for you on the way to the airport."

"Actually, I did bring a coat because I knew we would go to Wyoming," she said.

"The lady thinks ahead. Very good. Speaking of looking ahead, I'll go rummage in the kitchen freezer and see what I can find. Marline usually leaves casseroles for me at home, so there may be one or two here."

"I'll help," she said, walking beside him. She still fought the consequences of her wild kiss, which she couldn't take back, and she would have to battle her lusty urges all evening.

He found a pasta casserole that he placed in the oven, and she began to make a tossed green salad. "You have everything here. This place is as well stocked as a grocery."

"Speaking of well stocked..." He came up behind her to slide his arms around her waist and nuzzle her neck.

She smiled and turned in his arms to grip his forearms and stop him. "I did not say one word about well stacked and you know it. And we weren't going there, remember?" she said, too aware of the breathlessness of her voice. He was too close, still holding her, his green eyes melting her resolve.

"You started this outside."

"I was proving a point," she said while she fought to

maintain space between them. Her gaze lowered to his mouth.

"I didn't get it. Show me again," he said in a husky voice.

She slipped away from him. "You got it totally. Now get back to fixing dinner."

Shaking his head, he reached for glasses for ice water.

They worked companionably for a few moments, him setting the table and her tossing the salad. When he spoke, she was surprised to find his mind on business.

"Your brother has some property that will come on the market. He said he would call me when it's available and I can take a look at it."

"Are you expanding your office?"

"No. I'd fix up the building so that I can lease it to another business. Sloan's good to call me when he gets those opportunities. If he doesn't want them himself."

"Sloan's done well in investments. He has a mind for math and figures. He did Dad's income tax for him until I graduated and could take up doing it." She tilted her head to study him with curiosity in her expression. "Buying a building to lease doesn't have much to do with your energy company."

"I'm diversifying," he said with a smile. "So you have that family math ability, too? I know Sloan has it. So does your dad. That's good."

"It comes in handy on the bookkeeping side of this business. Otherwise I'm far more interested in history and furniture and other things we deal with."

Soon she had the salad ready, and they sat at the kitchen table to start on that while they waited for the casserole to heat.

They continued to talk, all through dinner and beyond. Before she knew it, the hall clock chimed ten o'clock. She had promised herself she'd leave him then, but minutes turned into hours and it was two in the morning before she noticed the time again.

"Jared, I have to get to bed," she said. "I was going to go hours ago."

"But you were having far too good a time to leave," he drawled with amusement in his expression.

She smiled in return. "I suppose I'll have to admit I was."

"We'll do it again tomorrow night, because we'll be out on my Wyoming ranch and it's thirty miles to the nearest restaurant or bar. If you wanted dinner or dancing, you should have said so here. Although we'll be back."

"This was perfect tonight," she said, amazed at how much she'd enjoyed the evening.

He walked upstairs with her and at the door to her suite, he pulled her swiftly into his arms, leaning down to kiss her. His mouth covered hers firmly, possessively. She wanted to protest, to stop him, but the moment his mouth settled on hers, her objection died. She held him and kissed him, wanting more in spite of telling herself to walk away.

"Jared," she finally gasped, stepping back slightly, her hand on his chest.

"You started this earlier," he said, giving her a smoldering look. "For one second tonight, do you think I forgot or really cooled down? I've been wound up all evening, wanting you and trying to keep my hands to myself." He placed his hand against the wall behind her and bent close to her. "Now you owe me for getting me all stirred up. I intend to collect on that, Allison."

"I think you just did. Go for a midnight swim. See you in the morning," she said, slipping into her suite and closing the door. She let out her breath. Desire was an all-enveloping cloak that she could not shed. She should not have let go and kissed him passionately, because it had steamed both of them. He was not the only one still hot and bothered, aching for more.

In just hours they would go to his Wyoming house, and then return to Houston to finish this job. As soon as she did, she would get back to her ordinary life in Dallas. And maybe she should think about Phillip's proposal—something solid and safe with someone compatible. Would marriage be so unhappy without this wild, burning lust?

She stared into the dark, glad she couldn't see her reflection in the mirror. Her eyes would give away the answer to the question she asked.

Though she prepared for bed, sleep was elusive. Jared filled her thoughts. He slept beneath the same roof. She could easily make love with him. Would it cool her burning need or just bind her to him irrevocably? She already knew the answer. It was hours before she fell into a fitful sleep with nonsensical, disturbing dreams.

Jared woke early and hurried to the heated pool. The morning air was chilly, and he walked fast, shedding a beach towel and dropping the others he carried to leap into the water. He came up and began to swim laps in long strokes while his thoughts were on Allison.

He couldn't get out of his thoughts that moment when she had moved over him, tossed away her shirt and gave him those wild kisses, or her declaration that he was missing out on the best part of life—the intimacy and joy of marriage and family, of making love when he wanted.

She hadn't convinced him about marriage and lifestyles, but he had been captivated by her more than ever. Sexy, beautiful, intelligent, she was becoming a close friend. They were compatible in so many ways, yet different enough to keep things interesting. But it was the fact that she could always surprise him that added to her charm. From that first night six years ago when she was in college, she had surprised him. He didn't know what to expect from her, and that hadn't changed at all.

Allison was special. She had warned him that he might fall in love. Could she be right? She was unique, with so many good qualities, but that ability to surprise him dazzled him because he didn't think he could ever tire of being with her.

He stopped swimming, breathing hard, treading water and lost in thoughts about her. Maybe he should fly back to Dallas and get out of her life before he was the one to be hopelessly ensnared and his visions of mountain climbing and all the other things he wanted to do went out of his life forever. He glanced at the house and thought about her in bed, asleep.

"Oh, hell," he whispered. He wanted her in his arms. He wanted to make love to her more than he wanted anything else. She had him tied in knots. If he didn't want to fall irrevocably in love, he'd better run fast, yet he didn't want to say goodbye to her yet. Far from it. He swam to the edge of the pool, climbed out and grabbed the beach towel to wrap himself in, then grabbed a bath towel to dry his hair. Slipping on flip-flops, he headed for the house.

Later in the day they flew to Wyoming, where Allison was captivated by the winding streams and the breathtaking mountains with snow still on the peaks. Even so, spectacular scenery could not fully capture her attention with Jared seated close beside her. At the airport, a car waited with a driver, a cowboy named Rocky Long who worked for Jared, and he held the car door open until they were seated.

"This is beautiful country," she said to Jared. "Do you spend a lot of time here?"

"No. I thought I would, but I don't. I come in July sometimes, or August, depending on what's happening."

"It's gorgeous scenery."

"I agree with you on that one," he said in a deep voice. She glanced at him to see him turned, his back to the car window. He faced her, a faint smile on his lips.

She ignored him and turned back to her window, yet now she was far more self-conscious, aware of her deep blue sweater she had brought from home and the jeans she traveled in. She had her hair in a long, thick braid that hung down her back. The air was cool and crisp, and she had pulled on a lightweight navy jacket.

It was an hour's drive before they finally wound along a ranch road, and his sprawling three-story home built on the side of a mountain came into view. Though the road had been cleared, snow piled along the sides and weighed down the branches of tall spruce trees. Finally his house came back into view. Smoke rose from two of the chimneys.

When they got out of the car and she crossed the back porch, she looked at an arrangement of rockers and a porch swing that gave the appearance of a family home instead of a bachelor pad.

The moment they stepped inside, delicious smells assailed her, and she inhaled deeply. Rocky said he would get their luggage while Jared took her jacket to hang on a hook in the wide back entry hall. He hung his coat beside it and took her arm. "Come meet the rest of the staff. They live on the grounds and take care of the place as well as work for me when I'm here."

They stepped into the kitchen. "Allison, meet Daphne Long, Rocky's wife. Daphne, this is Allison Tyler."

"I'm glad to meet you. It smells wonderful in here," Allison said.

"Vegetable soup. I hope you like it. I have a roast cooking, too, and an apple pie, so there should be plenty to eat around here."

"C'mon," Jared told her. "I'll show you your suite and around the house."

While rustic with log walls and wide plank floors, the house was inviting and filled with antiques. A fountain splashed in the wide front entrance and two matching curved staircases with black iron rails swept up to a second floor. All the rooms were large with floor-to-ceiling windows that gave striking views of the area.

They climbed the stairs to the second floor and entered a suite that held a large sitting room and stairs leading to another story.

"This is your suite. The bed and bath are upstairs."

"The view from here is wonderful. This is a beautiful home, and you barely live in it. That seems a waste."

"I enjoy it when I'm here. Come see where I am. Tonight we'll be alone, and we'll build a fire and sit up here, because I have the best view from my suite. Right before the sunset, sometimes it takes your breath away."

She followed him down the hall, seeing another facet to him now—the man who had so much yet could still enjoy a sunset. She was glad because she had thought maybe he had to take risks to get a thrill out of life.

They entered another sitting room not far from hers. This one was larger, and she was instantly drawn to the wall of glass that gave a view even more breathtaking than he had indicated. "Jared, it is magnificent here. I don't see how you can leave it," she said, looking at sunlight glistening on the snow-covered peaks of tall mountains. Dark pines covered the slopes. She could see a pond not far from the house and a stream running through it, then across the meadow away from the house. "The land is gorgeous," she said. "Far more than I expected."

"I'm glad you like it here. I always think it's beautiful," he said, standing close behind her. She could feel the heat from his body, and his voice was deep and quiet.

"I'd think you'd stay here all the time," she answered, forgetting the view and thinking about Jared, closing her eyes as his lips brushed her nape.

"I appreciate it when I'm here, but I love Texas. Besides, I do have a company to run."

His breath was warm on her neck, and he stood close behind her, his hands rubbing her shoulders lightly. "You're the first woman I've ever brought up here."

Startled, she inhaled deeply. "That surprises me. And it means you're here very little."

"More than you think. Now I'll remember you were here with me."

The conversation at the moment was not going the direction she thought it should. "Jared, we might as well start looking through your house. The sooner we do, the quicker we'll finish," she said breathlessly.

"You're in a major rush to finish this job and get away," he said, his warm breath blowing lightly on her nape, tickling, tantalizing and as light as a caress.

"That's what we came for."

There was a moment of silence, and then he stepped away. "Whatever suits you, we'll do. We'll go down and have lunch first while Daphne is here. We may get some hot corn bread."

Allison gazed into his green eyes and couldn't move. Desire was tangible, hot, pulsing between them. With a deep breath she moved away, trying to put distance between them while gulping air as if she were drowning.

"Let's go to the kitchen, Jared." Her voice sounded deeper, strained.

She turned to glance at him, and he came forward to catch up with her. Together they walked back to the kitchen, and she was relieved to have Daphne in the room with them while they got their lunch.

They ate in a cheerful yellow-and-white breakfast room adjoining the kitchen. An expanse of windows framed another spectacular view that competed for their attention with the steaming bowls of vegetable soup served by Daphne.

After lunch they begin to walk through the rooms that were less formal, but still held marvelous antiques and interesting relics of early-day life in the West. She was surprised that his Wyoming house was as large as his home in Dallas.

Before sundown, Jared stopped her. "That's enough for today. We're already half finished with this house. Daphne and Rocky are gone, so we're on our own tonight. Daphne has a roast with vegetables in a cooker and a casserole in the freezer that I can heat up. What's your preference?"

"Definitely the roast."

"Good choice. I want to clean up and change, so I'll meet you in the library in an hour. We'll have a drink before dinner. Then afterward we can watch a movie if you want."

"I may just look at the scenery and enjoy the fire."

"Sounds good to me," he said.

When she stepped into her suite and closed the door, she leaned against it. She felt as if she had been fighting a silent battle all day. Every time Jared was present, she had to struggle to avoid flirting with him, to avoid responding to his flirting, to keep a distance from him. Just his mere presence disturbed her. Each time he flirted or touched her, it was more difficult to curb her response to him. She didn't want to think that she'd be with him for possibly another week.

She went in to shower, her thoughts monopolized by Jared and the evening ahead. The days with him were beginning to go beyond lust. Jared was turning into a friend she could talk to for hours on end. The friendship was far more dangerous to her than the hot passion because friendship was deeper. She had to finish this job soon, or she would be in love with him.

Her life was totally wrapped around family and business. The only man in her life was Phillip, who had already offered marriage—several times. A marriage between two like-minded people. A lifetime in a marriage that would never hold the breathtaking excitement she found with Jared. Love might come if she married Phillip, but it would never be this heart-pounding, breath-stopping dazzle she experienced with Jared.

As she dressed for the evening, she wondered about two things. Could she continue to resist him?

And did she really want to?

# Seven

She found him downstairs in the enormous kitchen. Music played, a blues number that was background music but made her think about dancing. Enticing smells filled the room. The table was set in the breakfast area, and he had glasses of red wine poured and ready.

Jared stood with his back to her, and her gaze drifted slowly over his broad shoulders, covered in a plaid woolen Western shirt, down past his tight, slim jeans, all the way to his boot-clad feet. Drawing a deep breath, she fought an urge to walk up behind him, press against him and wrap her arms around him.

Instead she sedately entered the kitchen and kept a wide space between them. "Hi," she said quietly. "Good music. May I help you?"

He turned, his gaze flicking over her. Putting down a knife and an apple, he rinsed and dried his hands. "Just peeling an apple. The music is a motley assortment." He closed the distance between them to place his hands on her waist. "You're definitely the most delicious thing in this room," he said in a deep voice.

She inhaled and thrust her hands into her pockets so she didn't reach for him. "Thank you, I think. I'm sure I can do something here."

"Oh, you can do a lot of things," he drawled. "The first on the list—"

"Not that sort of thing, Jared. I'm sure I can help get dinner," she interrupted swiftly, unable to keep from smiling at him.

"It's impossible to avoid me, us. Let go, Allison. You're fighting yourself more than you're fighting me," he whispered, gazing intently at her.

"Shall I pour water for dinner?"

He held her with a gaze that grew more intense. Her heart drummed because she thought he would kiss her. Instead he walked away to pick up two glasses of red wine. "Let's have our drink first." He held one out to her, and her fingers brushed his as she accepted it.

"We can sit where we have a view," he said, motioning toward the adjoining sitting area.

She went ahead of him. A fire crackled in the fireplace, the orange flames dancing high while the setting sun glistened off the snowy mountain peaks. "This night will be difficult to forget," she said, thinking about the scenery and the fire, but mostly about Jared. The slight contact was a magnet pulling on her senses. All his casual touches were constant reminders of the excitement, the fabulous sex they could have together.

"I won't forget it, and I hope you don't. Not any of the hours we've spent together."

She smiled at him. "When we part, we'll both start forgetting."

"Have you forgotten the night we met?"

"I'll take the Fifth on that one."

"That's an answer. A big answer and a satisfying one. Neither have I."

Truthfully she remembered every minute, every second of that night. Just the mention of it had her heartbeat racing, her mouth drying. She'd give anything to experience another night like that. But she couldn't.

Because this was a dangerous conversation, she tried diverting it with a question.

"Are you always able to take off work as much as you have since I flew to Houston?"

"Not at all, but this is different and something I need to get done."

"I can do this job without you."

"I know you can. I assure you I'm keeping up with the important issues in the office remotely. But I want to pick out furniture for both my homes, and I want to be with you—therefore, I spend my time each day with you. You're doing a great job."

"Dad is the brains of all this. I'm learning."

"Is there anything that scares you about the job?"

"Sure—missing something incredibly valuable. Giving people the wrong information, which I try very hard to avoid doing. I'm scared that Dad will want to retire before I'm ready to go on my own, but if he wants to retire, then I want him to retire. Being on my own really scares me, but he will always help as long as he can."

"I'm guessing that you worry more about his health than any of those things about your job. After all, you are related to Sloan, and you're bound to have some of that worrywart in you."

"You're right about Dad. I'm more concerned about his health than anything else. He's getting older, and I know it. I suppose that's one reason I want to marry. I want him to know my children. I want them to love him the way I do."

"My dad will never know his grandchildren. Too late now." He shrugged. "Don't know if there will even be any. Maybe someday."

"I feel a biological or some kind of clock ticking in my life for that reason."

"You won't run out and marry that Phillip fellow just to get married, will you?"

"Now, what difference could that possibly make to you?" she asked, smiling, amused by his statement because he couldn't possibly care.

"Maybe because if you're going to get married, it should be for love."

"You have to make the best of what life presents you."

"Tonight life has presented me an opportunity to share a gorgeous view, a roaring fire, a delicious dinner, maybe a dance or two and some wild kisses with the most beautiful blonde I've ever known. Here's to a great evening," he said, raising his glass in a toast.

"To a great evening—with or without all of that. And thank you for such a blatantly exaggerated compliment, but nonetheless, I enjoyed hearing you say it."

The music changed to a fast number and Jared shoved a table out of the way, moved two chairs and then came over to take her hand. "C'mon. Dance with me."

"Jared, we weren't—"

"Live a little, Allison," he said, smiling and still holding out his hand.

The music was as tempting as Jared, weaving a spell, making her want to dance while his green eyes coaxed. She took his hand and stood, falling into step with him as they danced to a fast number. She had dropped his hand and danced around him, watching his sexy moves, hearing his boots scrape on the polished floor. As he twisted and watched her, tension increased. She could feel sparks crackle in the air around them. Her body hummed with need that increased every minute she watched him.

The next piece was even faster, rock music from another era, but an old favorite of hers. As they danced to the enticing beat, she could feel some of her pent-up frustrations relaxing, and she let herself go. When he came close to her, his hips bumping hers, she felt her desire build.

The song ended, and he caught her wrist lightly. "Come on. We'll get our drinks and have dinner."

In a short time, she faced him across the table near the fire. The succulent, tender roast fell apart. But she had lost her appetite. Jared was being his most charming, and the evening was turning into a night she would never be able to forget.

All through dinner he entertained her, and afterward he built up the roaring fire again.

"Jared, look at the moon," she said, standing by one of the windows to look at the huge white ball over a mountain peak.

"If you want to see a real view without climbing one of the mountains, come with me," he said. She followed him as they ascended the stairs to his suite.

She remembered the breathtaking view from the sitting room in the daytime. But it couldn't compare to what she saw at night: the outline of dark mountains, their snow-covered peaks glistening in the moonlight against a sky holding myriad stars that she'd never seen in Dallas or Houston or in any city.

He turned on a light and led her to a spiral staircase. She took the opportunity to look at the furnishings in the sitting room: a mammoth television, an antique desk and armoire, a suit of armor in a corner that she suspected was authentic. Two matching thick Oriental area rugs covered the polished plank floor. Upstairs, they went through a loft-style sitting room that overlooked the downstairs and on into a bedroom with a canopied king-size bed. Logs were stacked in the fireplace as they had been in his sitting room below.

"I'm going to build a fire. We'll want it shortly." He

pushed a button and music played, this time an old song that she loved.

"We're not where you can see the spectacular view yet. That was my primary goal in this location for a home." He paused to get two coats out of a closet and held one out to her. "We're going outside. You'll need this."

She shrugged into it. "I hope we're not climbing out onto the roof," she said, amused and wondering where he was taking her.

"No. I have a balcony off my bedroom."

They walked out onto a large balcony with a wooden railing. A light wind blew and cold air enveloped her. Taking her hand, Jared led her up a few more steps to a higher level of the balcony that held two chairs and a table.

"Now look."

She was already taking in the vast world spread before her. Moonlight spilled over the mountains and, far below, meadows. The moon's brightness caught silver glints in dark ponds when the wind stirred wavelets, and the sky twinkled with what looked like a million stars. Jared stepped close behind her, wrapping his arms around her. He was warm, shutting away the cold.

"It is so beautiful," she said, knowing far beyond the spectacular view, she would remember most of all the tall, exciting man holding her close. Turning in his arms, she looked up at him.

"You know I can't forget this," she whispered. "You're not going to forget standing here with me, either," she added solemnly. "I'm here, Jared, and I want more from you. If that scares you, you'd better run," she said softly.

She wrapped her arms around him beneath his coat while his hands slipped beneath hers to pull her close inside his open jacket. Warmth from their bodies banished the chill. Desire was a blanket of warmth that heated and heightened temptation. This appealing man, who ignited sparks whenever they were together, had started the blaze, had fanned its fire, and she wasn't letting go without giving some of the heat back to him. She didn't intend for him to easily forget her, toss her into the history of women in his life. Standing on tiptoe, she kissed Jared full on the mouth, her tongue going deep as her body quivered with longing.

A blast of cold wind swept across the mountain, whistling through the pines at the end of the balcony and buffeting them. His body, his arms, his kisses shut away the cold. Bending over her, he kissed her passionately, making her want more. She pressed more tightly against his hard body.

Another blast of wind whistled around the house and became a deep sigh through pine branches while Allison pressed into him, kissing him hungrily. Desire fanned the longing, and Jared stood in her arms, showering kisses on her. She wanted him, and tightened her arms around him while she continued to kiss him. Memories came stronger than the wind, running over her, tugging at her.

"Jared," she breathed, pausing momentarily to look up at this tall man she couldn't resist. Awareness of him intensified. Memories of his hard body, his kisses and lovemaking taunted her, held promises of rapture, of bonding and release.

"Let's get out of the wind," she whispered.

He picked her up, holding her in his arms to go back.

"I can walk," she whispered as she wrapped her arms around his neck.

"I want you in my arms. I have to hold you," he answered, ignoring her remarks and carrying her inside to set her on her feet. He passed her, closing the door and locking it. She was barely aware when he shed his coat and hers, tossing them over a leather chair.

His gaze rested on her. Intense and heavy lidded, his green eyes held blatant desire that made her draw a deep breath. He wrapped her in his embrace, leaning over her to kiss her. The moment their lips met, she was lost to everything else.

Her insides felt as if she were in a free fall. She wanted to kiss him for the rest of the night. She wanted him with all the restrained longings, memories and dreams she'd had about him in the intervening years.

His tongue went deep while his hands moved so lightly over her. Desire unfolded and spread. She could not hold back. She decided to try to make him feel some of the frustration that she felt. He had flirted, teased, kissed and caressed her since he had walked into the Houston mansion. Jared was human—his heart was not locked away in a vault. Yielding to determination and desire, she let go of her resolve to avoid complications. He was capable of falling in love, maybe was more vulnerable than he thought. Jared was in her arms and she wanted him, wanted the intimacy, the fulfillment.

Smoldering and sensual, his green eyes made her breathing short. He pulled her sweater over her head to toss it away. Spreading a blanket on the thick rug, he turned to pick her up, carrying her closer to the fire. Once he released his hold on her, his sweater went next, and she inhaled, running her fingers over his broad, muscled chest. Urgency seemed to grip him as much as it did her. Along with clothes that were shed, her emotional barriers were flung aside. They stood with only the light from the fire spilling over them, a reddish glow that highlighted the planes of his hard body.

He was aroused, ready, drawing her against him to kiss her while his hands moved over her, drifting between her legs to touch her intimately.

Jared was in her arms once again. Years fell away and longing mushroomed. Thrills rocked her while she relished every kiss, each touch. Her moans were from exquisite pleasure, her gasps from fiery need.

His hands were everywhere until she pushed him down on the blanket and moved over him to trail kisses along his body, tasting the salty skin of his neck and going lower.

She caressed his marvelous body. And he let her, winding his fingers in her hair and propping his head up with the other hand to watch her only seconds before he groaned and pulled her into his embrace to kiss her.

He picked her up to place her on the blanket and come down between her legs. She watched when he opened a packet to put on protection.

"Jared," she whispered, rubbing his hips with her long legs. "Jared, come here."

"Darlin'," he whispered, an endearment she loved. Then he filled her, slowly, and in minutes his control was gone. Urgency drove him, and she clung to him, moving with him. Need for him coiled into a tight spring. He was slippery with sweat from loving, hard, his muscles bulging, his perfect body making her want him more than ever.

Sensation enveloped her, lifted her until she crashed, spinning out in rapture that was total. "Jared," she cried, holding him as if he would vanish.

Pumping, he shuddered with his release, sensations still bombarding her until finally they both slowed, gasping for breath.

Gradually she became aware of things beyond Jared. The fire burned steadily as a log crackled and fell, sending a shower of orange-red sparks up the chimney. The low flames spilled heat over them while the thick blanket and carpet beneath them cushioned them from the hard floor.

He rolled over to keep her close with their legs entangled. He showered light kisses on her temple, her throat.

"Perfect, love," he whispered and she turned her head a fraction to kiss him, stopping him from speaking, wanting to savor the moment and keep the world and words shut away.

He showered kisses over her, caressing her with feathery touches. "Allison, you're the best," he whispered.

She smiled, stroking his smooth back lightly, winding her fingers in his thick hair, relishing every inch of him pressed against her. Memories of the past moments thrilled and dazzled her. "I wish I could say 'abracadabra,' and you would always remember this night when you go out on your balcony or, even better, when you're in here."

"I'll remember. I remember the night we were together before. I recall it in great detail." She traced his lips with her finger, and he turned slightly to kiss her hand. "This is perfect, Allison. I'm glad you're here with me." He propped his head on his hand and looked down at her, combing her long hair away from her face with his fingers. "When it's daylight, we'll go out on the end of my balcony again, and you can see what a spectacular view I have. But it's not nearly as good as the view in here right now."

"I need a sheet or my shirt or something to have a shred of modesty."

"Oh, no, you don't. I want to look and touch and kiss you all night."

She smiled at him and hugged him lightly. "So does this ranch of yours have a name?"

"Of course. River Bend Ranch. Very original," he added drily. "The brand is a combination of RBR."

"Sounds original to me. Is there a river?"

"Sure. Allison, when this job is over, can you take a

weekend to come back up here with me? It'll be later in the spring and even prettier by then."

"Let's not talk about the future yet. I don't want to think about tomorrow."

"That's fine with me," he said, lying down again on his back and pulling her close against him. "In a few more minutes, before my side is toast, we'll get up. We can shower together or run a tub of hot water. What holds the most appeal for you?"

"The tub of hot water sounds fabulous right now."

"Then that's what it'll be. Let's go, and I'll show you my big bathroom that cost a fortune to build."

They stood, and she caught up the blanket to wrap it around herself beneath her arms. He looked amused. "What are you doing?"

"Trying to be modest."

"I think you tossed modesty aside an hour ago. We're getting into a tub together, too. No room for modesty there. Or are you wearing that blanket into the tub?"

"Of course not."

"Then you don't need it now. Do you want me to cover up?"

She moved closer and ran her hand over his backside and then up his chest. "Oh, I don't think so," she replied in a breathless, sexy voice. "No. This is definitely a spectacular view," she said.

"I know a far more enticing sight." He unwrapped the blanket from her and tossed it away. Then he picked her up to carry her.

She wound her arms around his neck and kissed him lightly. "Has it ever occurred to you that you might fall in love someday even if you don't intend to and don't want to, and it will upset all your plans for adventures?"

"I don't think that will happen. I think I've made that clear to anyone who has an interest in a future together."

"You might not have total control over love."

"Of course I do. Everyone does."

"You think?" she asked, amused by his certainty he could control falling in love. "Now maybe you're flinging a challenge my way."

One dark eyebrow arched in speculation. "Maybe I am. Try to make me fall in love, Allison. We'll see if I can resist."

She laughed softly. "That's a challenge I think I will let drift right on past. I'm not out to capture your heart," she said, her words stirring a twinge of guilt.

"If any woman could, it would be you."

She looked at him, suddenly solemn. "I won't be the one. I couldn't take the life you lead. Not in someone I deeply love. Each time you walked out the door, it would tear me up inside." She smiled. "Jared, darling, you're quite safe from my seductive wiles," she stated in a sultry voice, running her fingers along his jaw.

"You keep that up, and we'll never even get to the tub," he said in a deep voice that had lost all amusement.

"Oh, my. I didn't know I could do that to you. What else can I do?" she teased, always enjoying flirting with him.

They entered his bathroom that was actually two large rooms, one with mirrors, plants, a massage table, a wingback chair, a rack of magazines and a flat-screen television. In one corner was an enclosed shower.

She followed him into another large room with a stand holding folded fresh towels and a large sunken marble tub. He began to run water, turning back to look at her, a tantalizingly slow, thorough perusal that had the same effect as caresses would have.

"Jared," she whispered, stepping closer to him.

He was aroused, studying her now with hunger in his eyes.

"We just made love. We have a tub of hot water waiting. C'mon." She took his hand and they climbed into the tub. He turned off the faucets before they sat. He pulled her between his legs and she reclined back against his warm body while hot water swirled around them.

They talked, and when the water cooled, he added more hot water until she finally raised a hand in front of his face. "Look, I'm withering."

"I don't think you're withering. Let me see," he said, cupping her breasts to run his hands lightly over her. His hands were warm, the water making their skin slippery as he slowly caressed and stroked her.

"Jared," she gasped and wriggled away slightly, rubbing against him with each move she made.

Standing, she splashed water, stepping away from him. He stepped out of the tub and pulled her close as they began to dry each other with thick, fluffy beige towels. He was aroused again. His green eyes had darkened with desire. He framed her face with his hands and looked down at her before he kissed her.

Stepping close, she slipped one arm around his waist to hold him while her other hand ran over his shoulder and down his back. His arm circled her waist tightly, and he drew her closer as they kissed.

It was hours later when he pulled her close against him, and she put her head on his chest.

"I'd say we fit together rather well," Jared murmured.

She felt his warm breath on the top of her head as they lay once again on the blanket before the fire. They had made love again, but it still wasn't enough.

"When we get back to Texas," he asked her, "will you

come to the rodeo with me? You won't be scared I'll get hurt. It's not that wild and woolly."

"Of course it's that wild, or you wouldn't be doing it. Yes, I'll watch you ride, but if you get hurt, you'll never bring up the subject of going again."

"That's an easy promise, since we may not see each other in the future. Sure, I promise," he said lightly.

His words dissolved the euphoria she had been enveloped in. The reminder of her future without Jared was a cold dash of reality that she'd hoped to put off until morning. It was knowledge she knew full well but hadn't wanted to think about it tonight.

"Jared, why do you take such risks? Why are you drawn to so many wild sports?"

"I like the challenge, the discovery. It seems incredibly exciting to think about climbing Mount Everest and seeing that spectacular landscape. Life is filled with marvelous adventures that are thrilling, and I want to do them all. I want to see and do and experience life."

"You remind me of my mother, of all people—sort of larger-than-life with a zest and hunger for adventure, living every moment to the fullest. She could get excited over a rose or over jumping out of a plane—which, by the way, she did."

"I knew a little about her but was shocked the first time Sloan started telling me more about her. Since you, your dad and Sloan are all worriers—your dad not as badly—I figured she was, too."

"Just the opposite," she said. "And my brother Chad was like Mom. He was the life of the party, always fun, always could cheer anyone up. He had loads of friends, and my mom was invited to a lot of parties, and she had loads of friends. They just seemed to wring more out of each moment of their lives, which was good because their lives were cut short," she added. "I'll always miss them."

He hugged her lightly. "Sorry. I know you will. That hurt dulls, but it never stops."

"I don't ever again want to lose someone I love because of something needless and risky."

"I understand that, but life was meant to be lived. You can't crawl into a bubble and shut away the world, so you might as well get out there and live. Watch out, Allison, you don't want to wake up someday when you're seventy years old and filled with regrets over the things you were scared to do. It's too late then. For a different reason, that was what happened to my dad."

"That won't happen to me."

"I hope not. I think you're missing out on life. You're observing, not living."

"So you think I've been an observer tonight?" she asked in slow breathy words while she drew circles on his flat stomach with her finger. He inhaled deeply and slid his arm around her waist.

"No, not tonight. Tonight you were thriving on life and its excitement. Aah, Allison, this is paradise. Maybe we can take an extra day or two to stay in Wyoming. I'll work on that. Perhaps if I occupy your time just right, you won't even get around to work for the next few days."

"You have tonight. That's for certain," she said lazily, trailing her fingers back and forth slowly over his muscled chest. "So what do you do in the rodeo? Calf roping, bronc riding?"

"I will ride a bull."

"Why did I even ask? You're thirty. Aren't you getting too old for that one? That's really a rough sport."

He grinned. "Come watch me and then decide whether or not I'm too old."

"Your confidence will get you through it, I'm sure."

"Challenges are exciting. If I can do it, then it gives me satisfaction, a sense of power, a feeling of accomplishment."

"A feeling of accomplishment, a challenge," she repeated. "I get that from identifying a piece of furniture in the correct century. That's not quite the same as risking your life riding a one-ton bull or climbing up the side of a mountain in a blizzard."

"I like physical challenges. I like a lot of physical things," he said as he rolled on his side and looked down at her. His eyes drifted slowly over her features as he studied her, making her heart beat faster. "I can't get enough," he said and his gaze lowered to her mouth.

Her lips parted. She slid her arm around his neck and pulled his head closer to kiss him. The minute he kissed her in return, her heart drummed and desire rekindled.

Dawn spilled into the room. Allison lay in the crook of his arm, Jared sleeping beside her in his massive bed, and gazed into the dying embers of the fire. They had made love repeatedly through the night. Each time probably locked her heart more securely with his. The night had been folly, yet something she no longer wanted to stop from happening.

What had last night meant to him? Another challenge met? Excitement, lust, fulfillment? Had it meant anything?

She turned slightly to look at him and his arm tightened around her waist. She expected his eyes to open, but they didn't. Was she in love with him already? She studied his features that still made her certain he was the most handsome man she had ever known. Also, he had turned into a friend. At the moment it seemed impossible to think that when she finished this job, she would tell Jared goodbye and not see him again. Right now she couldn't accept that, and today, she simply wouldn't think about it.

She ran her hands across his chest, pulled the sheet over them and closed her eyes, certain they would make love again before many hours passed.

It was noon when they returned to their task of deciding what might go into his house. She focused on the job, trying to bank desire and avoid thinking about their night or touching him now. He constantly flirted, sometimes lightly touching her, a casual brush of his hand, but after their lovemaking, the slightest contact was difficult to ignore.

Each time he distracted her she got back to business, until six o'clock in the evening when he took her iPad out of her hands.

"You've whizzed through this house and we've marked things to bring up here. Now it's time to quit for tonight." Before she could answer, his cell phone rang, and he took the call, walking out of the room as he talked, but she heard enough to guess it concerned business. She picked up her iPad and continued making notes.

To her surprise, he didn't come back for a while, and she moved on to a large dining room, taking a picture and making notes. Working alone, without discussing possibilities with him, she moved faster, going from room to room and getting enough done that she saw they could finish tonight if they went through the rest of the house after dinner. As far as she could see, there weren't as many things to go into the Wyoming home as there would be in the Dallas house.

She was in a bedroom when he finally appeared.

"Sorry, that was business. There's a company we've been trying to buy. They've made a counteroffer. I think we have something we can work with to get what we want, but it means I have to talk to some people right now. The kitchen is filled with food, so just help yourself. I'll have to put my dinner on hold."

"Want me to fix something for you?"

He shook his head. "I'm not hungry. I'll get something when I am."

"Jared, I'm making good progress. I can finish tonight, and we can go back tomorrow."

"That's good, because I'll have to get back to the office. I may send you and the plane on to Houston."

The twinge of disappointment was offset by the knowledge that it was for the best. She could work faster without him on some things; on others, it helped to know what he wanted to keep and what he didn't.

"Holler if you need me," he said and left, looking down at his phone to touch numbers and make a call.

She didn't see him again that day, and she finished touring the rooms where she thought he might want something from Houston. Some rooms she could merely glance at and tell that nothing would fit in with the decor.

She hadn't been particularly hungry either, and put off eating, finally getting a glass of milk and a couple of cookies, and heading to her suite.

In the morning, after she had dressed and clipped her hair up on the back of her head with a few tendrils slipping free, she went down to the kitchen. Hunger had finally set in.

She could smell the coffee before she entered the kitchen, and she heard Jared talking. She wondered whether he was on the phone or if someone was there with him, but when she entered, she saw he was alone, talking on his cell. He sat in the breakfast area with a mug of steaming coffee. He wore the same clothes he'd had on the night before. His shirttail was out, his sleeves turned back. A dark stubble covered his jaw and his hair was a tangle. Papers were spread over the table in front of him.

She poured orange juice and coffee, adding thick cream to her mug. She got out butter and bread to make toast, and scrambled some eggs so there would be enough if Jared wanted any.

He finally finished his call and put down his phone. "Sorry and good morning," he said, smiling at her. "You look great," he said. "I'd come give you a hug, but I don't think you'd want me to."

"You didn't go to bed last night."

He shook his head. "No, too much to do. I've had things faxed to me that I had to read and sign."

"I scrambled some eggs for us, and I have toast. What else can I get you?" she said, setting two full plates on the table. "I poured orange juice for you, and I found some preserves."

"I'm famished."

"I'm hungry myself. So are you buying a new company?"

"We're getting closer to acquiring it, and I'm at the point now where people who work for me will take over for a while and deal with this. There were just things I needed to make decisions about, and time was of the essence."

"That's all right. You don't need to explain. I finished looking at this house. I have my notes and pictures, and I'm ready to return to Houston and finish there."

"Anxious to get rid of me?" he asked, with a crooked grin.

"I would never say that," she replied.

He shoved aside papers and waited as she sat. "I'm glad you went on to your room last night, because by the time I looked for you, I decided you might be asleep. I've already made arrangements for a flight to Dallas this morning at ten o'clock because I need to get back. I can send you and the plane on to Houston, or if you prefer, you can stay in Dallas through the weekend and we'll both go to Houston on Monday."

"I'll just go on to Houston and finish. After all, I was hired to do a job."

"I don't mind if you wait."

She shook her head. "Thanks. I'll go to Houston," she repeated, resisting the temptation to stay in Dallas. It was the sensible thing to do and the practical choice.

"Last night, did you decide what I might want to have moved here?"

"There's a mahogany bookcase that I think would be perfect in your library. It could go along the wall opposite the fireplace."

He nodded as he drank his juice and ate a piece of toast.

"That octagonal mahogany table could go in the study. My guess is that it's eighteenth century. Dad will research it if he doesn't know."

"Good choice."

She ran down a list, and he nodded after each one.

"You agree on all this?" she asked, looking up. He had finished eating and was watching her. The moment she looked into his eyes, her mouth went dry. Those depths of green held so much desire, she trembled, aching with want.

Electricity filled the air while heat spread in her and longing became tangible. Locked into his stormy gaze, she could barely breathe. Her heart pounded and every inch of her wanted his touch.

Standing, Jared pushed away his chair and walked around the table. Disheveled, a night's growth of beard on his jaw, he had never looked more desirable.

# Eight

"We lost a night together," he said, stopping close to her. "Too bad I need a shave and a shower." He took her hand to draw her to her feet. Her chair scraped as she stood, while her heart pounded.

He pulled her to him. "I don't care," she replied, slipping her arms around him. He leaned down to kiss her, his beard rough, the woolen shirt soft beneath her fingers as she kissed him.

Urgency rocked her. Swamped with desire, she wanted him with a desperation that was mirrored in his actions. Clothes were tossed away, and in minutes, as they feverishly kissed and touched, he picked her up.

Wrapping her long legs around him, she clung tightly while they kissed. Right there in the breakfast room, he lowered her onto his erection, filling her in one dazzling motion. Sensations bombarded her. The blaze of desire raged out of control. She wanted him. Wanted his loving because it could vanish from her life after this moment. Her roaring pulse shut out all other sounds. She cried out in a climax, ecstasy pouring over her while he thrust wildly, reaching a pinnacle and crashing as she had.

Rapture enveloped her, and she held him in her arms. The rough stubble of his beard scraped her cheek. She raised her head to look into his eyes and see the satisfaction she felt.

"You're very special," he whispered, and her heart lurched. His words were spellbinding. She gazed back at him, and the truth hit her, hard and fast. She had fallen in love with him. She might as well face her feelings. What she did about them was another thing. If he fell in love, could she deal with his lifestyle? Why worry about it now? They weren't at that point yet.

She lowered her legs, and he set her on her feet. "I should shower," they both said at the same time and smiled.

"This time we'd better do it separately," he said. "I need to get rid of this beard that's started and clean up."

She grabbed up her clothes, yanking her big sweater over her head that covered her to her thighs.

"Aw, shucks," he said as he watched her. He had pulled on his shorts. He walked over to put his arm around her and kiss her tenderly. "All I want to do is hold you close."

"We'll shower. We have a full day if we expect to get back to Texas."

"Yeah, I need to, but that isn't what I want. Allison, this is great," he said, kissing her lightly. The look he gave her started fires again—it was the warm look of a man in love, whether he declared that love or not. She refused to think about the complications love could bring to both of their lives. Instead she held her clothes in one hand and wrapped her other arm around his waist to walk beside him as they went upstairs.

At the door to her room, he kissed her again, a kiss that began tenderly and changed to passion when he dropped his clothes at his feet and held her against him.

Finally she stepped away. "I think showers are in order. I'll see you shortly."

His breathing was ragged while he stared at her as if debating whether or not to leave her. Wordlessly he scooped up his clothing and left. She closed the door to her suite behind him and headed for her shower for the second time that morning.

They were flying to Dallas first, where it would be far warmer, and later to Houston, which was even warmer, so she dressed in jeans and a long-sleeved red cotton shirt, knowing she could roll up her sleeves if needed.

In Dallas, when the plane taxied to a stop, Jared stood and held out his hand. "I'm going to miss you," he said.

"You'll be way too busy," she replied in a breathless voice, hating to part with him.

"Never," he said. "I'll come to Houston as soon as I can." He kissed her goodbye and left the plane. A car met him on the tarmac, and he turned to wave, then climbed into the car and was gone.

She missed him already and could only wonder how it would be when the job finished. Would Jared try to continue to see her? As quickly as the question came, she faced the truth that she couldn't continue to see him because of their differences. When the job ended, she needed to end the relationship.

All during the flight to Houston, she thought about their lovemaking the previous night and this morning, already wanting him, yet knowing it was best he was in Dallas. Finally the plane landed in Houston, and soon she was back in the mansion to finish her task.

Late in the afternoon she returned to the upstairs study to look at an early eighteenth-century Italian library table, carved on all four sides with four drawers. She ran her hand along it. She had been surprised that Jared didn't want it, but he said he had one in Dallas that was similar and he didn't want another.

She wanted it in her living room and loved its ornate carving, but if she told Jared, she suspected he would just give it to her. It was far too valuable, and she didn't want him doing that. When she had sent a message to her dad that she wanted to buy the table, he had commended her on her beautiful choice.

She wished Jared was back beside her, already missing him and everything about him. The following Friday was their date to go to the rodeo. Would she be able to watch Jared without the anxiety she felt watching Sloan when he had ridden in the bronc event?

Every night Jared called her and they talked, sometimes for hours. Each day she missed him more than the day before, something that she hated to acknowledge. And then Wednesday arrived, and she finished with his mansion in the middle of the afternoon. On the next call from Jared, she informed him and soon arrangements were made for her to fly back to Dallas that night.

"I'll meet you at the plane," he said.

"Jared, I won't get in until eight."

"Then that's when I'll see you, and I can't wait. We'll go to my house, and if you want something to eat after you land, I'll have it."

"No, thank you. I'll eat an early dinner."

"See you tonight, darlin'. I have to run. I have an appointment that I'm already five minutes late for."

"Goodbye," she said, shaking her head but thinking about his endearment. Did it mean much with him? She had no idea.

Jared drove to an older part of Dallas where he had grown up. Big homes were set back on well-tended lawns while stately trees lined the streets, their branches sprouting new bright green spring leaves. He turned into the drive of the Tyler house, memories assailing him of spending hours there with Sloan. He recalled one time when it had snowed—a rare event in Dallas—and he had gone home with Sloan. When they had stepped out of the car, he had been hit in the chest with a puny little snowball and heard female giggles coming from behind a nandina bush. Sloan had had a snowball hit his feet, and he had glanced at the bush in disgust, looked at Jared and they had both scooped up snow to quickly pack snowballs the size of tennis balls. Sloan had run to the right and let one fly, hitting one of the girls who had been behind the bush. She screeched and ran. Jared had thrown a snowball and hit Allison in the face. She'd thrown one back at him, lobbing it with a wild swing, hitting his chest.

"My bratty sister," Sloan had said. "Let's get her."

Both of them had scooped up more snow while Allison did the same. "She's outnumbered, besides a few other advantages we have, like being twice as big," Sloan had said. They'd both hit Allison with snowballs but she'd thrown a few back. Sloan had scooped another handful and had run toward her.

She'd flung one more snowball at him, hitting him in the face as she turned to run, her long yellow pigtail bouncing when she ran. He'd let her go, waiting for Jared. "Be glad you're an only child."

"Frankly, I've been glad of that many times and some of them are because of your little sister. Let's get the snow off your drive, and we can shoot baskets."

Jared smiled now at the memory. He would never have believed then that someday he would be interested in Allison. He would have taken any kind of bet on that one. He had paid little attention to her and thought of her always as Sloan's bratty little sister, which was what Sloan often called her.

After he and Sloan went to college, Jared rarely saw her

and never after Sloan's wedding until that magical night when she had been eighteen.

He could hear the chimes, and soon Herman Tyler swung open the door. He looked older than he had the last time Jared had seen him. His pale blue eyes were like Sloan's, and they bore a definite family resemblance.

"Come in, Jared," Herman said, shaking hands and welcoming him. "It's good to see you again."

"You're looking good, Mr. Tyler," Jared said. "I'm glad you're feeling well."

"Yep, knock on wood. For now I am. What brings you by? Want to see the preliminaries on the catalog?"

"No, sir."

"Want a cold beer?"

"Thanks, that would be nice. I've talked to Sloan lately and saw his latest pictures of his family."

Herman laughed. "My son always has 'latest pictures' of his family. They must have a million pictures already. Little Megan knows how to pose and Jake, the baby, has already learned to smile when he's told to."

"Cute kids, and Sloan seems crazy about them." Jared followed Herman into the kitchen and in minutes accepted a beer.

"Let's go to the study," Herman said. "I have things I've brought from the office in there. You have some fine furniture in that Houston mansion. I'm sure you know that already."

"I do, but I don't know how fine or which is more valuable. I know what I like, and I've told Allison."

"Have a seat, please."

They sat facing each other, and Jared sipped the cold beer. "The reason I wanted to see you, sir, is to talk to you before Allison gets back home and is with you all the time."

"Now I'm curious."

"She told me there are a couple of items in the mansion that she would like to buy. She will not tell me which ones, because I'm sure she suspects I will give them to her."

"So you want to know which pieces?"

"Yes, because I want to give them to her. She's done a great job, and she's a friend—your whole family is like a family to me. I know if I leave it up to her, she won't let me give them to her. I suspect you know what she wants, so please take them out of the sale and mark them for her. And I'd really prefer to surprise her, so she doesn't fuss with me about it."

"Jared, I know what she wants, and they're very fine items, worth a lot. Are you sure you want to do this? You're paying us quite well."

"I'm sure. This has nothing to do with paying you for the job. I'm doing what I want to do."

Jared gazed back while Herman Tyler stared at him with curiosity in his expression. Finally Herman nodded. "Very well. I'll tell you what she wants. I have the pictures I've pulled anyway, so we can watch for these two items through the sale. I'll get the pictures."

Jared waited, even though he didn't particularly care which things she wanted. He had already selected what he liked. But he had a feeling it was important to Herman.

Herman returned with two pieces of paper in his hand, which he handed to Jared. One item he recognized immediately as a library table he had given some thought to and decided to let go. The other was a gilt wood mirror with gryphons at the top.

"This is an expensive mirror, Jared," Herman said. "That's a sizable item to give as a gift, and I suspect she will return it to you."

He smiled at Herman. "I'll convince her to keep it. I'll get a truck to pick them up as soon as she leaves Houston and then have them delivered to her condo."

"I'll be amazed if you get her to keep them."

"Mr. Tyler, is there anything you would like? I'd be very honored, sir, to give it to you."

"No, there isn't, Jared, but thank you. That's a touching offer." He looked around and waved his hand at all the antiques in the study. "I've already had one heart attack that was serious enough to make me stop and look at what I have. I've been trying to thin things out, because this house is filled with the accumulation of a lifetime. Thank you, though, for your generous offer."

"If you change your mind, please let me know. I'd make the same offer to Sloan, but I've seen pictures of his contemporary house, and he and his wife are definitely not into this type of furniture."

Herman chuckled. "No, they're not. My daughter-in-law just looks at my home and shakes her head. I think she would be happy to help me get rid of half my possessions, and she doesn't understand Allison liking old furniture at all."

"Well, it keeps the world an interesting place. Does Allison have these two pieces tagged in any way?"

"I'm sure she did tag them. She put her name on them instead of mine, and they each have an identifying number. The library table is 142 and the mirror is 207."

"That's all I need," Jared said, sitting down again to talk to Herman for the next half hour. Finally, he stood. "Thanks so much, Herman, for the help. I really want to do this for Allison."

"It's extremely generous. Almost too generous."

"No, sir. She earned it. I'm real happy to be able to do this. Now, it's our secret for the time being."

"Sure. Want another beer?"

"Thanks, but no. I should go."

Herman followed him outside and stood on the front step. As Jared started down the driveway, he turned back to wave. When he got in the car, he glanced at his phone in a pocket between the car seats. He couldn't help the disappointment when he saw there had been no call from Allison.

Jared thought about their night together in Wyoming. He wanted Allison with him all the time. Could he get her to move in with him? Until their night in Wyoming, he hadn't thought he had a chance of that, but now he wondered. She seemed as eager to make love as he was. He wanted her with him, in his arms, in his bed every night. He missed her all through the day now, and the nights were empty and lonesome, something he had never felt before in his life. How had she become this important to him? Why was she so different from other women he had known?

She would be home tomorrow night. Jared's pulse sped up at the thought, and he wished she could be here tonight. He couldn't wait to see her. When had he become so ensnared by her that he couldn't wait for her to appear?

Allison ran to pick out what she would wear home, finally selecting jeans and a pink shirt. Anticipation hummed while she grew more eager to see Jared with each passing hour.

When the plane left Houston, she never looked back. Finally it taxied to a stop in a Dallas hangar. A black sports car was parked inside, and Jared came forward while her heartbeat raced.

She stepped out of the plane and walked to meet him as he came toward her. She forgot their surroundings or that anyone else was in the hangar. She let him sweep her into his embrace, leaning close to kiss him, a devouring kiss that made her want to be alone with him more than anything else.

"Come on," he said, his voice sounding hoarse. "Let's get out of here. Someone is getting your things."

The drive seemed like it took forever, and she kept her hand on his knee while she told him about finishing, and the most interesting pieces of furniture or items she had found the past few days.

Truthfully, she wasn't even certain what she said to him. Her joy over seeing him shocked her because she hadn't expected this bubbling excitement to grip her. An undercurrent of worry dimmed with each second. Jared was here, bigger than the threats to her peace of mind right now. She wanted him, and desire, hot and constant, over-rode caution. That could come later.

At her condo, the moment they stepped inside and closed the door with the lock clicking into place, Jared pulled her into his arms to kiss her.

They made love through the night. As the sky grew lighter with dawn, Jared tightened his arm around her. She lay with her head on his chest, her hair spread over his shoulder. "Move in with me," Jared said in a husky voice. "I want you with me like this."

Her heart lurched. Her first reaction was to say yes, to share what they had and hold on to it. She wanted to be with him. These past few days she had missed him far more than she had dreamed she would. It seemed her love for him grew with each day. Move in with him and he might not want her to ever move out.

"Did you hear me?" he asked, shifting to his side to prop his head on his hand and look down at her.

"I heard you, and I'm thinking. Jared, you're alone.

You've lost your dad now. You have close friends, but you're alone. I'm not. I have my dad and my brother."

"Darlin', I can take care of your dad if we need to. Right now you said he's doing well, and he sounds well and as full of life as ever."

"He may sound that way, but he's changed. He's more frail than he used to be. And I can't ignore Sloan."

"No, but you don't have to let him live your life for you. He's not your parent. He's a brother, and a worrying one at that."

"I know. I just have to think about it because that's a big step. It's a commitment. Actually, a huge commitment for me."

"Yes, it is," he said solemnly. "It's a commitment for me, too. You take my breath away. You were all I could think about. You've interfered in my work because you weren't here, and I was so busy thinking about you that I couldn't concentrate."

She laughed softly. "I don't think so, Jared. Besides, you just got another woman out of your life."

"I'm not making that up about you interfering in my work," he said solemnly, toying with her hair with his free hand. "As for Dawn and any other woman in my life, I have not asked anyone to move in with me. Not ever."

Shocked, she sat up to look at him. "Are you telling me the truth? Why would Sloan tell me you have so many women in your life?"

"I don't think it's as many as your brother tried to indicate, but I didn't ask any of them to move in with me. I may have lived at their place—which may be splitting hairs to you, but it isn't splitting hairs to me. This is far bigger," he said, giving her a direct look that sent a streak of fire to her toes.

"Then I'm surprised," she said, her mind reeling over his request.

"Frankly, I'm a little surprised myself. You do something to me," he whispered, reaching up to kiss her.

She placed her hands on his broad shoulders while she kissed him in return. Finally, he paused, his gaze drifting over her features. "I may be falling in love," he said gruffly, and her heart thudded.

"But you don't know?"

"What I feel for you has never happened before." Her heart pounded, and she kissed him passionately.

Later, he wound long locks of hair around his fingers, pulling gently. "Can I take you to dinner tonight?"

"Sorry. Dad has already asked me to come over. He's cooking. I'm sure you can join us if you'd like."

"Since it's your first time to be with him in a while, I'll wait. Next time I'll take you up on it. Of course, it will bring Sloan on the run."

"He probably wouldn't even know."

"Are you going to work tomorrow—actually, today?"

"I'll tell Dad I'm exhausted and I'll be in in the afternoon. So you'll have to shuffle off then."

"I'll disappear then, but right now I'm here, and I'm going to make the most of the moment." Drawing her closer, he leaned down to kiss her.

All afternoon while she worked, she thought about Jared. An inner debate raged furiously, and she could argue for either side whether to move in with him or not. Give in to passion and what she wanted, move in with him—that way, he might not ever want her to move out. Would he fall in love if they were together longer? Or fall in love if they were deep in an affair?

On the other hand, he wouldn't change his pursuit of wild adventures. His life would be at risk continually. She couldn't cope with that. She was torn between the choices. She'd give him an answer Friday night. If she could accept watching him in the rodeo, then she'd try moving in with him and see what happened.

Friday afternoon she left work early and went home to dress for the rodeo, her eagerness to be with Jared churning in her. She had lectured herself to not worry about him tonight because he was doing what he loved, and he could take care of himself.

She changed twice, finally settling on light wash jeans that had blinged hip pockets and a snakeskin belt with a silver buckle. She wore a black Western shirt and let her hair fall freely around her face. As she brushed her hair, the doorbell rang. She glanced at the clock. "You're early, Jared," she said to no one, hurrying to the front door and thankful she had given herself plenty of time to get ready.

Expecting to see Jared, she swung open the door and stopped abruptly. A stranger in a uniform stood at her door. At the curb a truck was parked. Another man in uniform stepped out of the truck and went to the back to open double doors.

"Delivery for Ms. A. Tyler."

"That's me, but I didn't order anything. What kind of delivery?" she asked, wondering what the two men could have in the truck. Puzzled, she looked at the clipboard in the man's hands.

"We have two boxes, one table and one mirror, picked up yesterday in Houston."

Shocked, she nodded and signed where he showed her. "Who sent this?"

"J. Weston."

"Bring it in," she said, dazed, her curiosity growing. Jared was giving her the two things she'd intended to buy from the Delaney mansion. How had he known what she wanted? The only person who'd known was her father.

Surprised over the gift, she motioned to the men where to set the boxes inside her front door.

Accepting a copy of the receipt, she closed up behind the deliverymen as soon as they left. She couldn't wait for Jared to get there and ask him about the boxes.

Twenty minutes later when she opened the door to let him in, she lost her train of thought. He looked so good, he could have been in an ad. His black wide-brimmed Western hat sat squarely on his head. He wore a black Western shirt, jeans and black boots. Stepping inside, he pulled her into his arms. "I've waited all day for this moment," he said, kissing her long and hard.

Longing filled her, a deep hunger for him as if she hadn't seen him for weeks. His kiss held dreams and fiery reality, a start to seduction.

"Jared," she gasped finally. "You're going to be in a rodeo tonight. We should go."

He was breathing as hard as she was, and his eyes were half-lidded, making her weak-kneed and wanting to forget the rodeo completely. "All right," he said with a rasp. "We'll go."

"Before we do—thank you. The things arrived from Houston today. You shouldn't have done that. Let me pay for them."

"No, I want you to have them. I didn't even see those boxes when I came in. I was too busy looking at you."

"You found out what I wanted from Dad, didn't you?"

"Yes. Have you opened them?"

"No. You'll probably have to help, because they look as if they are really packed well."

"I'll do that, but not right now."

"I didn't mean now." She stepped up to wrap her arms around his neck. "I shouldn't accept those from you without paying you for them."

"You have to. I won't take payment."

"Thank you," she said, standing on tiptoe to kiss him, another long kiss that became passionate and made her forget the evening ahead. His arms circled her waist, and he held her tightly.

She finally stopped. "We have to go."

He inhaled deeply, looking as if he might be debating whether to make love or go.

"Jared, you can't be a no-show," she said.

He nodded. "We'll take up later where we left off," he said. He took her arm to walk out to his car, closing the door when she was seated and walking around to climb behind the wheel.

"Are you excited over your ride tonight?"

He glanced at her as he drove. "Over my ride? No. I can barely think about it. I'm excited, but not over that. My excitement is over hot kisses and your soft body. Your big blue eyes and your mouth on mine. Over expectations of holding you later and making love to you for hours tonight. Over dreams of having you with me tomorrow night and the next night."

"I get the picture," she said, smiling at him. "I'm trying to avoid thinking about when you have to ride one of those monstrous bulls."

"I'll have the time of my life for maybe eight long seconds, I hope, although there are some other things that are definitely more thrilling."

"I can't believe you'd want to come out riding an animal determined to get rid of you that wants to stomp you into the ground or worse."

Laughing, he reached over and squeezed her hand. "I do other things that are more fun. This comes under one of those exciting challenges, just to see if I can do it."

She shuddered. "I think that's a guy thing."

He laughed again and held her hand as they drove.

At the arena, they walked into the big hall, past vendors while Jared greeted people he knew. And then he paused. "Well, look who showed up," he said, and Allison recognized a familiar face as Ryan Delaney walked up to them. In a brown wide-brimmed Resistol, he was another handsome cowboy in the arena. Brown hair showed beneath the hat and his dark brown eyes were lively above his wide grin.

"Hi, Allison," Ryan said.

"You two know each other?" Jared asked, glancing at Allison who smiled in greeting.

"Yes, we do. Back since my college days," she said. "It's a small world."

"Well, Ryan and I have a burger bet on tonight's bull riding. Soon I will be having a burger dinner, compliments of Ryan," Jared said, grinning.

"I can tell you right now, I'm going to want a big stack of onion rings with mine."

"You order whatever you want, and I'll order whatever I want, and you will pick up the tab because I intend to beat you tonight."

"We'll see. I expect a different outcome."

"You two need to start teaching self-confidence seminars," Allison remarked.

Smiling, Jared draped his arm across her shoulders. "I'll see you later," he told Ryan.

"Oh, yes, you will. It was good to see you, Allison. You have to put up with a lot," Ryan teased, glancing at Jared, whose grin widened.

As they parted and walked away from Ryan, she fanned her face. "No hand-wringing, 'I hope I do well' words between the two of you. I'm not certain I've ever been so deep in confidence and bluster. Well, maybe with the little boys I knew back when I was eight years old."

He chuckled. "Ryan and I like the challenge, and the bet just adds a little more satisfaction."

"Have you ever lost to him?"

"Oh, yeah. And he's lost to me. It's in fun. Ryan's good, and I like to beat him. Actually, he's really good. He's won the most."

"Well, it's refreshing to hear you admit someone might be a smidgen better at one of these wild things you do," she teased.

"Wait until this is over and we're back at your place. I'll show you what you and I both do best," he said in a deeper voice, leaning close to her ear.

She smiled up at him. "Now I want this evening to be over soon."

"So do I, Allison," he said, suddenly looking earnest with his smile vanishing. "I want you in my arms. If I could, we'd turn around and leave right now."

"You can't skip out now," she said.

Jared led her to a box seat. "Bull riding is the last event. I can sit with you until later in the evening."

They sat together, and for the first few events, she enjoyed the evening and Jared beside her. Desire was a steady flame simmering in her, making her count the minutes toward the end of the evening when they would go back to her condo.

When it was time for him to leave her, he turned to kiss her briefly. She gazed into his green eyes and saw excitement, and she realized times like this were essential for him. She watched him leave, wanting to go with him, knowing she couldn't, and she wouldn't like it if she went back to watch him get ready to ride.

She wondered if she would be able to watch or would have to close her eyes. Right now she wanted to leave. Tonight would be a test of sorts for her—her reaction to watching him would indicate how deeply her feelings ran for him.

Thinking about the excitement in his eyes, she took a deep breath and tried to calm down, reminding herself that he was doing what he loved to do.

The bull riding started, and the first cowboy came out of the chute. He was tossed from the bull in four seconds. Her hands clenched in her lap and she sat straight, fighting the fear that kept rising in her. Why did Jared have to have these thrills? He had given her reasons, but she still couldn't understand taking chances like the cowboys that she was watching.

The second rider barely hung on for three seconds, but the third rider almost made it, thrown off at the seven-second mark. But while the clowns ran toward him, the bull charged the rider and gored him. She felt lightheaded as she watched the clowns try to distract the bull, and then the animal turned to chase a clown. The cowboy lay on the ground and rolled over. A clown stood by him until men ran out with a stretcher. The second clown ran to help the first one keep the bull distracted.

She watched in horror as they loaded the cowboy on the stretcher and carried him out.

And then it was Jared's turn.

The announcer told the crowd about Jared's wins in the past, an impressive record that brought applause and cheers. She could see his black hat in the chute, see him on the bull. She had seen enough bull riding on television and been to enough rodeos that she knew what was happening in the chute as he wrapped his hand so he would be secured to the two-thousand-pound animal.

And then the chute opened and a huge gray Brahma bull leaped out.

# Nine

Allison watched in horror as the gray bull twisted and turned, leaping into the air while the announcer talked. She didn't hear anything the announcer said. All she could do was stare at Jared. He held on with one hand and the other arm whipped about as the bucking bull kicked out his hind legs relentlessly.

As she watched Jared, her world came crashing down.

She couldn't move in with him, live with him, grow to love him even more. She couldn't take this wild, risky life of his. Memories of the horror of losing her mother and one brother still haunted her, the senseless tragedy, the numbing shock, the terrible loss of two family members she loved so deeply.

The buzzer sounded, the ride was over and Jared had ridden for eight seconds. He jumped off and ran for the fence as the bull turned to chase him. A clown darted out, waving his hat while Jared jumped on the fence and climbed swiftly. The bull turned to charge the clown, catching the hat and tossing it high into the air.

She felt clammy and cold. Thinking about Jared's life, she hurt all over. She couldn't deal with a man who lived life in the manner Jared did, and now was the time to end it. She had been in euphoria about him, turning a blind eye to the life he led while he helped her with her inventory, made love and took her dancing. But that was just one facet of him. This other facet of him terrified her. She couldn't live with it.

She had to go back to her quiet, ordinary life. Go back to evenings with her dad and Phillip or one of her friends.

Jared suddenly appeared, and she couldn't keep from standing and throwing her arms around him to kiss him. It was kiss of relief, of joy he wasn't hurt, of goodbye.

For one startled moment he was still, then his arm circled her waist and he kissed her in return until she finally stopped.

"Congratulations."

"Let's go home."

"You won't know whether you won if we leave now. Don't you need to stay?"

"Not really. I'll find out later who won. Come on. This is what I want to do."

He took her hand and looked up at her, frowning. "You're freezing."

"I'm all right now," she said.

He put his arm around her, and they left. She was quiet on the way to the car, and once inside, he switched on the heater until the car was toasty warm.

He took her hand as he drove. "You're still cold."

"I'm all right, Jared. I'm warm. My hands are just cold."

"You worried about me, didn't you?"

"Yes, I did. I can't keep from that. I hope the cowboy who was hurt is all right."

"I heard he has a broken rib and a few cuts and bruises, but otherwise he's okay."

She was silent, and Jared became quiet, too. When they entered her condo and she had closed and locked the door, Jared reached for her. "I'm fine, Allison. I did what

I wanted. I didn't get hurt, and it was exciting. Stop worrying about it."

When he pulled her into his embrace, she was powerless to resist. Her resolve to simply walk away from Jared crumbled before him, and the words withered on her lips when he claimed them in a kiss. She didn't object when he picked her up to carry her to bed.

It was hours later when she finally gathered herself to tell him of her decision.

"I can give you an answer about moving in with you," she began in a shaky voice.

He looked down at her, anticipation flaring in his eyes. She steeled herself to deliver the blow.

"I can't do it. I want marriage with someone who doesn't put their life in danger at every opportunity. We're opposites in too many ways, and I can't deal with the terrifying daredevil risks that you thrive on."

"Allison, this is a big step for me. I told you I've never asked a woman to move in with me before. That's a commitment of sorts."

"It wouldn't matter if you proposed tonight. When I watched you ride, it all came back when I got the news about Mom and Chad, the crash and their deaths. I remember the fear and the worry caused by their loss. I can't do it. I can't go through that over and over with you while you risk your life again and again. You live life your way, and I'll live mine the only way I can. There will be a woman for you who will be so thrilled by all the wild things you do. I'm just not that woman. I'm in love with you, but I can't take your lifestyle. I couldn't possibly tie my life to yours."

"Allison, you're tossing away happiness with both hands. Move in with me and take a chance. I'm fine. I'm careful. I've done a lot of risky things, but I do them the way they should be done—with care and planning."

"Care and planning didn't matter for eight seconds tonight."

"Well, maybe not so much when you're on an irate bull, but I'm careful. Don't throw away what we have because it's unique and special."

"You can talk until the sun comes up. I can't change how I feel about this." It was killing her to say these words.

"You and your brother are major worrywarts, and it will hurt you, just as it has Sloan, who has cut so many sports from his life."

"I seriously doubt if Sloan misses any of them or gives them a thought now."

They looked into each other's eyes, and she could feel the clash, see the determination in the jut of his jaw, hear his deep breathing while he stared at her in silence.

He reached for her. "You're going to let this fire we have between us die? It's special—you know it is. You'll never find it with anyone else, and neither will I."

"I'd say you're the one letting it go. There's a life out there far more important to you, and I'm not so sure what we've found is unique between us. You'll fall in love and so will I, and we'll never look back," she said sadly, her heart breaking. "I want marriage and a family, and you're not ready for that, Jared."

He pulled her into his arms to kiss her. For a moment she was stiff with resistance, but he continued to kiss her, his arm banding her waist while his hand caressed her, running lightly down her bare back. She couldn't resist. His kiss and caress brought desire to life, making her want only his loving, his hands, his mouth, his body. Her fears were forgotten, her breaking heart salvaged for now because she was aware only of Jared, and she wanted him with more urgency than before.

He was right: it was unique with him, and in truth, she didn't think she would ever find this fire and excitement with anyone else, but tonight had to be their last. It was just postponing the goodbye until morning.

For now, she closed her mind to everything except Jared and his loving.

She held him with her arm around his neck while she ran her other hand over him and kissed him with all the passion in her. Dimly, above her pounding heartbeat, she heard his groan, a low rumble in his throat while his arm wrapped around her waist.

They made love through the night, but it was a frantic, urgent coupling. When daylight came and sunlight spilled into the bedroom, she slipped quietly out of bed and went to shower.

When she returned, dressed in jeans, a pale blue sweater and flip-flops, he was gone. As she walked into the hallway, he emerged from the guest bathroom. His hair was wet, combed. He had slight dark stubble on his jaw, and he wore the same clothes he had worn last night.

"I'll help you open the boxes."

"We can open them later," she said, again feeling as if her heart was being ripped out. She looked at him intently, memorizing everything about him: his eyes, his mouth, his hands.

"I won't be here later," he replied. His words cut and hurt, but it was the answer she expected.

"Just leave them, Jared. I'll have Sloan help me. I'm not ready to move them yet."

He nodded. "Do you still have the same answer—you won't move in with me?"

"No, I won't," she said. "I can't do it, and I know that now."

"And I can't give up the life I have. That's who I am, Allison."

She followed him to the door, and each step hurt more. She was losing him. It was her fault, her fears that she couldn't overcome. She wanted a family, and she didn't want the father of her children off on wild, life-threatening adventures. Her mother had been fun, exciting, filled with life, full of exuberance and enthused over whatever she was doing. It had been wonderful when everything was going right, but none of it, the exuberance, the excitement, the zest for living, had been worth the cost—losing her life in a crash that had also killed Chad. Total confidence in themselves seemed to go with that approach to life. That just wasn't for her. She wanted someone safe, cautious and as conservative as she was.

At the door he turned to look at her, his gaze going slowly over her face. He kissed her, holding her so tightly she thought she might not get her breath back. He released her, picked up his hat and was gone.

She watched him walk to his car, watched him drive away, and she knew he was leaving her life forever. While she hurt, salty tears began to spill over her cheeks. "Jared," she whispered, hating that she loved him. For the next hour, all she could do was cry his name.

Monday morning she dressed and left for work, thankful for the other people in her life.

Driving to an area of shops on the fringe of a residential part of Dallas north of downtown, she turned into the parking lot and entered through the back. Their appraisal offices were opposite two large rooms in the back of the building with another even larger room for storage. She found her father in the front rooms set aside for displaying furniture, mirrors, paintings and objects they had for sale.

When she joined Herman Tyler in his office, she kissed him on the cheek. He sat behind his desk, his gray hair neatly combed. He wore a pale blue shirt with an aged navy cardigan.

"I got the library table and the mirror from Houston. I think you had a hand in that."

"Jared wanted you to have them," Herman said, studying her. "Want to talk about Jared?"

"Dad, he's out of my life. We said goodbye this morning," she said, her words sounding stiff even to herself as she looked away from her dad's perceptive stare.

"He must like you a lot to give you those pieces."

She shrugged. "Jared is immensely wealthy, so the money part doesn't matter."

Her father nodded. "You don't look so happy."

She smiled at him. "You see too much."

"It doesn't look as if saying goodbye to him was something you really wanted to do."

"We just have very different lifestyles. I watched him ride in the rodeo Friday night." She nearly shuddered at the memory. "He probably won the bull riding."

"So Jared still likes doing the wild things."

"Too wild for me."

Her father put his arm around her. "Honey, are you sure you're all right?"

"Yes, I'm sure," she answered, smiling at him. "Now, let's get to work here," she said, looking at pages of pictures and descriptions spread on his desk.

"I'm putting more of the catalog together. You can start looking through the new pages I have and see what you think. You're in charge of the mailing list."

"I'll start getting it ready today."

* * *

All day it was difficult to concentrate, and her thoughts kept returning to Jared, but she expected to get him out of her mind soon and be able to work without thinking of him constantly.

When Phillip phoned her at three o'clock, she was in the front with customers, so she walked across the room to take the call and speak softly. When he asked her out that night, she accepted. She was swept away by an undercurrent of pain that flowed through her without warning. How long would it take to get over Jared?

Before she went home late in the afternoon, she stopped at the door of her father's office.

"Phillip is taking me to dinner tonight. He said you're invited if you'd like."

"Tell him thanks, but I'll decline. There's a baseball game on TV that I want to watch, and frankly, I'm tired. Be sure you thank him for me, and you have a good time."

"I will, Dad." She blew him a kiss and left for home, having mixed feelings and missing Jared more than she thought possible.

He didn't call, and by the end of the following week, she felt he was out of her life for good.

After work one night, Sloan came by to help her unload the boxes. "Dad said Jared gave you these."

"Yes, he did."

Sloan studied her intently and she looked away, busying herself trying to take some of the fasteners out of the box.

"Leave that, Allison. I'll get it," Sloan said. Soon they had the container open and the table stood on the fallen box.

"This is a beautiful piece of furniture," Sloan said, running his hand along the satiny finish. "Jared gave this to you?"

"Probably his appreciation for the job."

Sloan looked at both pieces. "That table and the mirror have to be worth thousands of dollars. There must have been something between you and Jared."

She didn't deny it. "There isn't now. I can't deal with his lifestyle."

"No, you can't, because he's still the wild man doing wild things. Jared isn't ready to settle down." He started collecting the boxes. "Dad said you went to the rodeo with Jared."

"Yes, I did. Right now, I'm seeing Phillip, so don't start in on me about why I shouldn't go out with Jared."

"That's good to hear. You'll never regret that, Allison. Jared has never lost his wild ways, and I don't think he will anytime soon." He stopped and looked at her. "But you don't look happy."

"I'm fine. You're being a worrywart again."

"Okay, okay. I just want you happy."

"I am. I'm dating Phillip. I'll probably marry Phillip, so just relax. Phillip is my type of person. We're happy. We're compatible."

Her brother studied her intently until she turned away.

"At least you and Phillip are compatible and like the same things in life."

"I'm sure you're right. Phillip and I are going to dinner tonight."

"I'm glad. Tell him hello for me. Maybe we can have you both over soon. Of course, it's chaotic with the kids running around."

"It would be fun. I'm ready for my nieces and nephew to come for their overnight. I probably won't even recognize Jake. He must've grown so much since I went to Houston. And I can't wait to see the girls. They're always fun to have here."

"They love being with you. I'll tell Leah because I'm

sure she is more than ready to let them stay with you. That would be wonderful."

"How about Friday or Saturday night?"

"Let me talk to her, and we'll call you. Now, let's move this table where you want to put it."

"In the living room," she said, taking one end while Sloan got the other. "Okay, let's go."

In minutes they had it positioned just right, and Sloan was getting ready to leave. He paused as if groping for words. "I—I'm glad you're seeing Phillip. Jared isn't the man for you."

"Don't worry about it, Sloan."

"Well, I'd better run."

She followed him to the door. "Thanks for helping me get the table and mirror out of the boxes."

"I didn't help you hang the mirror. Do you want me to?"

She shook her head. "Phillip will. Thanks again."

Sloan climbed into his car, and she waved as he drove away.

She hurt, and she missed Jared, and now every time she looked at the table or the mirror, she would think of him.

Glancing at the time, she ran to get ready for her evening with Phillip.

In the past year Phillip had brought up marriage every few months. The next time he did, Allison decided she was going to accept. She couldn't deal with a man like Jared, but Phillip would give her a family, security and, hopefully, along with compatibility would come love.

As she dressed, she struggled to keep Jared out of her thoughts. Everything reminded her of him, made her think about him. Did he even care that she had gone out of his life?

The next day she received a call from her brother. "Will you be home after work tonight? I'd like to stop by for a minute."

"I'm going out with Phillip again. He has tickets to a play. But I'll be home till about seven."

"I won't keep you long. Also, I talked to Leah. What about keeping the kids Friday night? Leah's friend Nan has asked us to go to dinner with them."

"Sure. Let the kids sleep over. I'd love having them."

"That's great, Allison. We'll pick up Jake after dinner because he doesn't sleep well and he can be pure trouble, but if you want to keep the girls all night, that would be wonderful, and they will be delighted. You know how they love to be with you."

"It's mutual," she said, smiling. "I'm anxious to see all of them, and I don't mind keeping Jake all night."

"Nope. Not this time. There may be something later when we will be out of town, and I'll accept your offer, but not Friday. He'll ruin your night. I'll let Leah know and she can tell the girls. They'll have their little bags packed within the hour, I'm sure."

She laughed. "I'm glad they like to come over. I have some new paint books and paints. We'll have fun. I'll call them tonight and invite them myself."

"You're a good aunt. See you after five tonight."

She wondered what he wanted and thought maybe he was coming by to see if she had her mirror hung yet, which she did not. This weekend she would get Phillip to help her hang it.

She thought about her last evening with Phillip. She had enjoyed it, but it had been quiet, no sparks, no excitement, yet she'd had a nice time. Their good-night kiss had been bland, meaningless really. Did she really want to tie her life to Phillip's? She was certain he had the same reaction to her. Yet in so many ways, they could have a good life together. Phillip traveled a lot and would be away a good part of the time, so she wouldn't see him or deal with him daily.

He was wealthy and could provide a comfortable life, and he was willing for her to continue working with her dad.

Jared, on the other hand, would not marry for years—if at all—and he would continue his wild lifestyle that she couldn't take. He was out of her life, and she was through seeing him. Every time she thought about the two men, she always came back to the same decision—accept Phillip's next proposal of marriage.

She returned to work, adding to the mailing list and reading over the rough draft of the catalog her dad was still working on. Looking at pictures of the furniture, it was difficult to keep her thoughts from drifting. Memories assailed her: of talking with Jared about this chair or that table, of sitting on an antique settee, of Jared kissing her.

She would be relieved when they finished dealing with his things, when the sale was over and he vanished out of their lives completely.

After work that afternoon at her condo, she put away the snacks she'd purchased for the little girls and Jake. She had new toys for all of them that she put in sacks to surprise them. She was eager to see them, and Friday night couldn't come too soon.

She made a final round of the rooms in her condo and decided she still wanted the mirror to hang in her living room where everyone who came to visit would see it. She got out a hammer and a picture hook for Sloan because she was certain that was why he was stopping by on his way home.

When she heard his car on the drive, she went to her front door to wait for her brother.

"Hi, how did it go today?" he asked when he came in through her back door.

"Fine. Soon we'll be all ready for Jared's sale, which

he won't attend. Neither will you. I know Leah would not want a thing from this sale."

"No, she won't. She is very much a minimalist, with a love of clean lines and contemporary furnishings. You know I don't care."

"Yes, I do. I assume you're here to hang the mirror."

"Actually, no, I'm not. I want to talk to you."

Startled, she looked sharply at him. "What on earth about? Your family is all right, aren't they?"

"Yes, nothing like that." He pulled out a kitchen chair and sat. "I can hang the mirror for you, too, if you'd like."

"Want something to drink?"

"Sure. Iced tea if you have any."

"I knew you were coming." She poured two glasses and got out some cookies to set across from him.

"Now, what's on your mind?"

"I'm beginning to feel guilty, and I feel I'm pushing you into something you shouldn't do."

"You're not even making sense," she said, staring intently at him.

"Dad has told me that Phillip has proposed to you before. This came up because of the gifts Jared just gave you."

"Sloan, stop worrying. I will not marry Jared."

"That isn't exactly what's worrying me," he said. "I want to tell you that Leah and I are very much in love and very happily married."

Amused, Allison smiled. "I think we all know that. It shows a little."

"Marriage should be to someone you really love, with all the excitement that goes with that. I think you're going into a loveless marriage just because time is passing and Dad isn't well, and you know he would feel better if you were settled down. You may want marriage and a family, but I don't want you to do something that will put you into a loveless marriage that is doomed from the start, or if it succeeds, never has that spark that is so—" he paused, as if searching for a word "—so special."

"You're worrying needlessly."

"Listen to me. I'm not through. I think part of this is my fault."

She laughed. "Sloan, you're not at fault for anything I do."

"I think I may have painted Jared with a very dark brush. For years I've warned you to avoid him."

It dawned on her as to why she was sitting in her kitchen with her brother when he should be on his way home from work. "Sloan, stop right now and let me save you a lot of talking. It doesn't matter what you've said about Jared. It's definitely over between us. I went to the rodeo with him and I couldn't bear to watch. I was almost physically sick. I cannot tie my life to a man who lives on the edge."

"I've ridden in rodeos, and that's not the wildest risk on earth."

"You think?" she asked drily. "Eight seconds on a bull?"

"Well, it's a dangerous sport, but age is against him. He can't keep doing all the things he does."

"Your argument is as leaky as a sieve. And it is going nowhere with me. If I marry Phillip, I feel sure we'll be happy because we'll both be doing exactly what we want."

She gazed into her brother's blue eyes and could see the doubt and concern. "Sloan, I appreciate your interest and how you always look out for me, but I'm all grown up. You have three little children to look out for now. You concentrate on them. You're a great brother, but stop worrying about the man I marry. It won't be Jared anyway, because he doesn't want to be tied down. I'm not moving in and living with him without the whole commitment from him."

"Well, that part is good. Jared does have a rather bad history with women and walking out on them, but he's getting older and he's growing up."

"Oh, if he could hear you," she said, laughing. "That would give him a laugh. Go on home to your family. I know they're waiting, and Leah probably needs your help with the kids."

"I feel guilty because Jared is really a good guy. I wouldn't have stayed friends with him all these years if I didn't think so."

"I know," she said, standing.

Sloan came to his feet, too. "You think about what I said about him. He's a good guy, and I can count on him when I need to."

"I understand," she said patiently.

"By the way, I saw in the paper that he won the bull-riding event."

"That will only encourage him."

At the door, Sloan repeated himself. "Give him a chance."

"Stop worrying. Now you're worrying about just the opposite of what you were worrying about last week. Sloan, you're a world-class worrier. Go home and worry about them."

He grinned and left, climbing into his car and driving away.

She shook her head. "Sheesh. My crazy brother," she said to herself. "'Stay away from Jared. Go marry Jared.' Sloan is losing it."


Friday night Phillip joined her, and when Sloan brought his children in, Leah came with him. Sloan looked startled to see Phillip. Jake held his small arms out to Allison, and as soon as she had hugged both girls, she took Jake from Sloan.

"Phillip, if you're staying, you're a glutton for punishment," Sloan said.

"I like kids. I have six nieces and nephews and I see them often. They're all here in town, so this is nothing. It'll be fun."

"Crazy man," Sloan said in fun to Leah, who smiled at Phillip and Allison.

"Pay no attention to him," Leah said. "He's great with the kids. Although today has been a little trying." She said goodbye to the children and got ready to leave. "We shouldn't be out late."

Carrying Jake, Allison went with Phillip as they followed Sloan and Leah to the door while the girls ran for the toy box.

After pizza, later in the evening, Allison painted at the kitchen table with Virginia and Megan while Phillip sat on the floor playing with toy cars with Jake, who sat on a blanket with toys spread all around him.

"Phillip, if you get tired just tell me, and I'll trade with you or just take him, and you can go watch television."

"I'm fine. He doesn't look as if he'll wear out for another ten hours. When does this kid go to sleep?"

She laughed. "Jake's a night owl."

Virginia turned to Phillip. "Sometimes Jake stays up later than we do."

"Does he now?" Phillip asked, rolling his eyes. "He may put me to bed."

"I'll play with him."

"I'm kidding. We're having a good time, aren't we, Jake? I think he's happiest crashing the cars. If I can just keep him from chewing on them...."

"You have teething rings there," she said, watching

Phillip run his car around Jake's and play with her little nephew. It was obvious how much Phillip enjoyed kids. She thought how easily they could repeat this scene over and over if they married each other and had a family of their own.

She had made her decision to accept Phillip's next proposal. But now she couldn't help but wonder: Did she want to settle for a safe, loveless marriage?

And how long would it be before she forgot Jared?

# Ten

On Monday morning, Jared entered his office after being in North Dakota for the past week on company business. He sat going through his mail, and then turned to listen to his voice mail. He frowned slightly when he discovered he had three calls from Sloan.

Jared thought about Allison. He missed her more than he'd ever thought it was possible to miss someone. Too often memories crept up on him and he couldn't keep from getting lost in them. Any time he saw a tall blonde walking ahead of him, his attention was riveted until he was certain it wasn't Allison, although common sense told him that he was not going to see her in a chance meeting.

Skimming over his list of appointments, he decided he had time now to return Sloan's call. "Is the property available?" he asked his friend after they greeted each other. He figured that was why Sloan had left so many messages.

"No. I called because I want to see you. How about lunch today? I can't talk on the phone."

"Okay," Jared said, because Sloan occasionally came up with a very good investment for him.

They made lunch arrangements, and then Jared forgot Sloan until his secretary thrust her head into his office and reminded him of his lunch appointment.

Shrugging into his charcoal suit coat, he left, going to

a downtown restaurant that was beginning to fill with the lunch crowd. Sloan was waiting, and Jared joined him.

After they'd ordered burgers and got their drinks, Jared asked, "All right, what's so urgent? Property? A building? Stocks? You must have something hot on your mind."

"Actually, I wanted to talk to you about my sister. And to apologize."

Startled, Jared stared at his friend. "What about your sister? And what on earth would you apologize for? Well, maybe I can guess that one—sort of butting into others' lives," he said, grinning and giving Sloan a slight verbal jab.

"Jared, I'm worried."

"You were born worried."

"I have a wonderful marriage, so I know that when you really love someone, marriage is paradise."

Jared thought he had already heard it all from Sloan, but now Sloan had found a new worry. "That's nice."

"No, I mean it. When love is good, it's beyond description. I want that for Allison."

"That's nice, Sloan. What's that got to do with me?"

"I'm getting to it. I don't think that's what is going to happen. She told me that the next time Phillip proposes—and he will propose because he does so on a regular basis—she will accept."

Jared had known that, but he still felt as if he had received a blow to his middle. "I already knew that."

"I don't think she'll be happy or that marrying Phillip is what she wants to do."

"I can't do anything about your sister accepting some guy's marriage proposal. She knows what she wants."

"What makes me feel guilty and bad about this is that I think I've described you as a wild man who will never settle down. You're my best friend, the best man in my wedding, a great guy and I shouldn't have made you sound so wild and crazy."

Jared laughed. "Is that what this lunch is about? Cool it, Sloan. It wouldn't have mattered how wild and crazy you made me sound if Allison and I had been in love and wanted to get married."

"I know you don't want to marry, but you might rethink that a little. I'm telling you, I'm happier than I've ever been. Far happier. It's wonderful, kids with runny noses and all."

"Kids with runny noses don't exactly sell me on marriage," he teased. "I'm kidding. I'm sure you're happy," Jared said, smiling at his friend. "You're the best as far as friends go. Well, maybe you could worry a little less, but you're a great friend. Allison and I aren't seeing each other, and it doesn't have anything to do with you."

"I have the feeling that I'm responsible."

"You are definitely not responsible. Case closed. You haven't done anything to change our lives, so forget it."

Now if only Jared could forget Allison as easily.

On the way back to his office after lunch, he kept thinking about Allison and remembering that first night when she was eighteen, and how she had shocked and dazzled him. He had never forgotten her since. He thought about her sitting on his lap, telling him that he was missing out on life with his need for adventure instead of love. Real, deep, lasting love with commitment. With Allison, that was what it would be.

She was marrying another man. Every time Jared thought about her marrying someone else, he got a hollow feeling in the pit of his stomach. She wasn't even really in love with Phillip. Yet she would be if she made that commitment.

Jared thought about the things he liked to do that Allison considered so wild. The bull riding was one. The deep-sea diving, the mountain climbing, the white-water rafting. If he had second thoughts, he'd better come to a conclusion soon. Sloan had called for a reason, and Jared suspected she was on the verge of getting engaged any day now.

He walked back to his office, burning off some energy, trying to think clearly about his future. Which was right for him—giving up the adventures he loved or giving up the woman he wanted?

Could he ever get her to accept him the way he was and let go of some of her fears?

The night of the rodeo he remembered how she had looked white as snow after his ride. Her hands had been ice, even in his car with the heater going. She had true fears, and that night she'd looked as if she would be physically ill.

Could he make any sacrifices for her? And was that what he wanted to do?

Telling his secretary that he didn't want to be disturbed, Jared went into his office and closed the door.

Marry Allison? He had never seriously thought about marriage. But then he had never seriously been in love.

He loved her. The realization surprised him. He hadn't stopped to take a long look at his feelings for her. He had pursued her, enjoyed being with her, tried to develop a relationship, have an affair, but he hadn't stopped to really consider how deep his feelings went. And if he asked her to marry him and she refused, would it make it more difficult than ever to forget her?

Jared walked to a window to look across the Dallas rooftops. He had expected her to do something like this, but not so soon. He had thought she would take some time after leaving him and think over her future, wait a while to see if he pursued her.

Instead, she was going on with her life as if he had never been in it. Perhaps Phillip was urging her to say yes.

Jared kicked a leg of his chair lightly with his toe, feeling frustrated and wanting to see her.

He stared beyond the roofs of buildings, seeing green treetops on the edge of town, some patches of green downtown. Was he losing the love of his life by not acting? Could he watch her marry someone else?

He crossed to his desk to pick up his phone, but then he put it down and stepped away, staring at it while he was lost in thought about her. Allison had declared her love for him. Did it really run deep? Thinking she was out there somewhere, probably at her office, he turned back to the window. What was she doing now?

Allison sat in her office while her dad was in front with a customer. She sat at her desk, composing a letter to go with the catalog. Everything was moving along toward the sale in early summer. She expected a really good response to the catalog that was filled with beautiful items and fine historical pieces.

She heard footsteps in the hall and assumed it was her dad coming back for something and that the customer had gone. She heard a knock at the open door and glanced up. Her breath caught and held while surprise shook her. Jared stood in the doorway.

Her heart seemed to stop and restart at a faster pace while she inhaled deeply. His green eyes held her immobile.

The silence stretched, and her heart became a steady drumming. Deep down she felt an urge to run into his arms. Instead, she locked her fingers together in her lap out of sight below her desktop. "Jared. What are you doing here?" she asked, finally finding her voice, but her words were breathless.

"Your dad told me to come on back," Jared said, ignoring her last question. He stepped inside her office and closed the door.

She came around the desk to wave her hand toward two guest chairs. They both stopped where they stood only a few feet apart. Neither made a move to sit but stood facing each other in silence.

"So what's this about?" she asked him finally.

"I want to talk to you in private. I figured if I called you and asked you to dinner, you would just turn me down."

"You figured right," she replied. "There's no point in going to dinner together."

"Yes, there is. We can talk."

She barely knew what she was saying to him. He stood too close, looked too handsome and she had missed him more than she had believed possible. His riveting eyes still held her, and she wondered if he heard her pounding heart.

Her phone rang once and she didn't even look at it. When it became silent, she guessed her dad had answered in the front.

"That was perfect timing. That phone call is an example of why I want to take you out so we can talk undisturbed. I want to be alone with you, not at an office or some other place where we'll be interrupted. I want to pick you up and take you to my house tonight."

"I think we've said everything there is to say to each other," she answered, barely able to get out the words. She wanted to say yes. She wanted to be in his arms. She wanted the evening with him, but it was ridiculous to put herself through that agony, and she guessed that he wanted to try to talk her into accepting his lifestyle. She couldn't think of another reason for his presence.

"Jared, I won't move in with you no matter what you say," she stated flatly, hurting all over again, a raw hurt that was as terrible as the first time they had gone through this.

"That is not what I want to talk about," he said quietly. "One evening. That's not so much, Allison."

It was an eternity if someone hurt badly, she thought. "All right, Jared. I don't see the point, but come by my condo at seven."

"Thanks for doing this. We could just go now. You could leave your car here."

"No, you come by my condo."

He nodded. "I'll let you get back to work. I'll see you then."

She felt the invisible wall between them that had never existed before, not like this. She didn't know why he wanted to see her, because she hadn't changed her feelings about him. Instead of the usual excitement she had always felt with him, she just hurt because she couldn't see any reason to get together again except to repeat the final goodbye.

Even so, the sparks had still been there in that first glance, when she had looked up and faced him as he stood in the doorway. The mesmerizing draw between them was as present as ever, and his handsome looks still took her breath away. Those things had not diminished or changed one tiny degree. Would she ever get over him? Ever stop responding to him?

She drove home in a haze and showered and dressed in the same state. She selected a simple black sleeveless dress with a short-sleeved, high-waisted sweater that would be a light wrap later in the evening. She let her hair fall freely around her face, and she was ready about ten minutes before seven.

She heard his car and headed toward the front of the condo. Her nerves were taut, a deep eagerness gripping her that she could not ignore or get rid of despite of her best effort.

The bell chimed, and she swung open the door to once again be captured by green eyes that were filled with obvious warmth and appreciation.

# Eleven

"You look gorgeous," he said as he stepped inside, and she closed the door behind him.

"Thank you," she replied, trying to ignore her fluttering insides. "Come in and I'll show you where I put the library table. It's beautiful. Thank you again, Jared."

"I'm glad you like it," he said.

"I love it." They entered her living room. "I plan to hang the mirror on that wall above the library table," she said. "I haven't had anyone to hang it yet, but I will. Sloan helped me get the library table in here, and Phillip and I have been busy, so we haven't hung the mirror yet."

"Are those the only things you wanted? Now's the time to tell me."

"Yes. I don't have room for too much, but these are beautiful."

"I agree. Do you have the tools and hook to hang the mirror?"

"Yes. I've always got those things around."

"Where's your mirror? I'll help you hang it," he said, shedding his navy suit jacket and placing it over a chair.

She started to protest, and then closed her mouth and led him into her small dining room. The mirror was on a folded blanket on one end of her dining room table. Jared picked it up easily.

"Let's see where you want it."

"You may get messed up doing this now," she said, looking at his navy slacks and the snow-white shirt with French cuffs.

"Doesn't matter," he replied in an offhand voice. He followed her back into the living room.

"I'd like it centered over the table, so it can be the focus of the wall if I put other pieces around it later. I'll go get a measuring tape." She retrieved it and came back to find him waiting.

"I marked a tiny spot on the wall that I think is the center."

"What did you do, just eyeball it?"

He smiled. "Yes. We'll see how good I am. Hold one end of the tape." He moved to the other side of the table and looked at the length of the table and then measured half.

"You're right on the target," she said. "Good eye."

She watched as he put a hook in the wall and then hung the mirror, checking to make certain everything was tightly in place. She watched him work, which seemed so right.

"Jared, both the table and the mirror are beautiful. Thank you so much."

He placed the tools on a towel atop an ottoman and walked up to take her in his arms. The moment he touched her, a wave of longing swept her, making her feel empty and needy.

"Now you sound more like yourself," he said. "Allison, I've missed you, and I've been thinking about us. That's what I want to talk about."

"I'm going to marry Phillip."

"Have you told him yes?" Jared asked, a muscle working in his jaw.

She shook her head. "I haven't yet, but I'm planning on doing so the next time he asks me."

"Forget that, Allison. That's why I'm here." His green eyes darkened while he took a deep breath. "Darlin', I love you, and I want to marry you," Jared said, his voice husky.

His declaration of love was a warm cloak enveloping her and capturing her heart. Excitement rekindled, a churning, bubbling hope that made her feel she didn't dare breathe.

"Let's talk about this, Allison," he continued. "Come sit down." He released one arm, still holding the other lightly as they sat on the sofa, and he faced her with his knees touching hers.

"I've thought about us. I don't want to lose you." His declaration sounded heartfelt. More words to bind her heart to him and to make her listen to what he wanted. "Maybe I can give up the wildest things if you can put up with a few that I find really difficult to say I'll never do again."

"Like what, Jared?" she asked, not daring to breathe.

"I can give up bull riding and mountain climbing. There are a couple of things I really want to keep doing. Most of all my deep-sea diving, because that goes with the ship salvage hobby, and I don't want to give that up."

"Have you thought this through?" she asked, "You've been so set on doing those things. You've talked about disappointment later—"

"I've definitely thought it through," he answered in a deep voice. "What about the deep-sea diving—can you tolerate it?"

"I can live with that one, I think," she said, stunned they were discussing what he would give up and what he wanted to do. She was as surprised by his declaration that he couldn't get along without her. All this time she'd been home he hadn't called, tried to see her or anything else.

Had he been thinking all this through before talking to her again? She pulled her attention back to him.

"I love white-water rafting and, darlin', that isn't as dangerous as some of the other things."

"I can live with white-water rafting, Jared," she replied carefully, thinking about it and unable to believe they might work this out.

"What about skydiving and hang gliding?"

"I've done both and don't have any interest or inclination in doing them again. You can eliminate both of those activities. I think we've covered it. I ski, but you ski. Can you think of anything else?"

"What about bronc riding?"

"What about it? Does that scare you?"

She smiled at him, letting out her breath. "No." Her smile vanished as she stared intently at him. "You would give up those things for me, the bull riding, the mountain climbing?"

Then it hit her—the irony of it all. "This proposal is connected to your propensity for taking risks," she said. "In fact, this may be one of the wildest risks you've taken, Jared, this risk of giving your love and asking me to marry you."

He looked startled. "Maybe it is, but I've taken risks before, and I'll take risks again. I want to take this one with all my heart."

Her heart began to pound. "You didn't answer—what about the bull riding and the mountain climbing?"

"In a breath I'll give them up," he said. "I love you, darlin'. Allison, will you marry me?"

She felt as if shackles fell from her heart. "Jared," she said, letting out her breath while tears of joy filled her eyes and spilled over her cheeks. She threw her arms around him, catching him by surprise. They went down on the sofa with her on top of him, and his arm tightened around her waist.

Raising slightly, she looked down at him. "Yes, I'll marry you. Oh, yes." Joy filled her, spilling over and making her laugh. "Jared, I can't believe this. I was so certain it was over between us and I'd never be with you again."

"I was, too, for a brief time, but I don't want to be without you. I'm willing to make some sacrifices if you're willing to put up with the things we talked about and agreed on."

"You have a deal."

His warm green eyes filled with love. "I seem to recall a demonstration of the benefits of being married. Well, I'm counting on that."

She smiled at him. "Unzip this dress," she said in a sultry voice. As soon as he did, she stood, wriggled and let the dress fall to the floor. Smiling at him, she moved closer as he smiled in return. The moment changed, and passion became a raging blaze that burned away thoughts about anything else except loving each other.

Finally she lay in his arms, close against his warm, naked body.

"Jared, I am unbelievably happy."

"I hope so. That's what I want. I want to always make you happy. Darlin', you have absolutely no idea how much I need you."

"I hope so, always and forever." She thought of something and sat up to look down at him. "Jared, you'll never believe this. I have a surprise for you."

He looked amused. "What surprise? Could it possibly involve your brother?"

"Yes. Sloan feels guilty for telling me all these years how wild you are and to watch out for you. He said you are a great friend and he shouldn't have painted such a dark picture of you." She smiled. "You don't seem surprised."

"I'm not surprised, because your brother came by to see me. He told me that you were about to marry Phillip. He doesn't want you to because he knows you and Phillip are not in love. He apologized. He feels guilty for saying the things he did about me."

Jared grinned and pulled her down into his arms. "We'll have to call and tell him the news, and then he'll start worrying about us getting married. First we tell your dad. I've already told him I wanted to marry you and that I was going to ask you to marry me."

"When did you do that?"

"This afternoon when I went to your office. I saw him out in front first."

"He didn't tell me."

"Of course not. I wanted the proposal to be a surprise." He kissed her. "Allison, I'm the happiest man on earth. Let's have this wedding as soon as possible."

"So we can have a baby?" she asked, smiling broadly.

"No, so I can have you with me every night possible. Babies later—maybe not much later, but give me a month at least."

She giggled and kissed him.

It was after eight when Jared pulled out his phone. "Let's call your dad and Sloan, and then we'll order dinner."

He handed her the phone and she hit Speaker, then told her dad that she and Jared were engaged. Her father's booming congratulations sounded hearty and sincere. She promised to come over the next day with Jared. "Honey, I wish you all the happiness possible. I think that's wonderful. Jared talked to me, and he loves you very much."

She turned to smile at Jared and plant a kiss on his lips.

Next they called Sloan, and she switched on the speaker button again. "Sloan, this is Allison. Jared is with me. We're getting married. Jared said you told him to propose to me."

"I did no such thing. I told you you might be marrying the wrong man." She laughed as her brother sputtered and tried to tell her what he had said to Jared. Finally he just gave up and offered his congratulations.

"Thanks. After all, I think this is all your doing."

"It is definitely not my doing," Sloan insisted. "Jared has never done one thing he didn't want to since he got out of school."

"Not so," Jared said. "Thanks, Sloan. I did listen to what you told me."

"Good deal," Sloan said. "Allison, I'll let you tell the girls. Here's Virginia."

"Virginia, sweetie," Allison said, "I'm getting married. I want you to come to my wedding."

Virginia began to screech, and Allison held the phone at arm's length. "I think she's happy."

Leah came on the phone next. "Allison, congratulations to you and Jared." The screeching in the background became louder. "Both girls are so excited, and Jake is just yelling because they are. They're thrilled, and so are we."

"Thank you. I'll call you tomorrow when things are calmer. 'Bye for now," she said, breaking the noisy connection. She turned to Jared. "Well, the girls are happy. Now you have nieces and a family—so much more, Jared."

"I'm still astounded this has happened to me. You've been upsetting my routine life since the night I ran into you at that wedding reception."

"Have I really?" she asked with great innocence. "You live such a mundane, routine life."

"If someone had told me when I was sixteen years old that I would someday marry Sloan's bratty little sister, I probably would have run away from home and never seen Sloan again. What a scary thought that would have been then."

"At that age, I thought you were kind of cute, but awfully old. I do recall once getting you squarely in the face with a snowball."

"I've always said you have a naughty streak in you that comes out in lots of different ways."

"Do I really now?" she asked in a sultry voice, running her hand over her hip and licking her lips.

"Yes, you do, and I love it," he said, pulling her into his arms to kiss her.

# Epilogue

In early May, Allison stood with her arm linked with her father's as the bridesmaids walked down the aisle. "You look so beautiful, Allison," Herman said, kissing her cheek, and she smiled at him.

"Thank you, Dad."

"I wish your mother could see you."

She smiled at him again and patted his arm.

"I'm happy for you and Jared. Be good to him, honey. He's really in love with you."

"Maybe you'd better tell him to be good to me," she teased.

"He will be. I hope you're as happy as your mother and I were."

"I hope so, too, Dad."

"I'm proud of you and Sloan. You've been great children, both of you."

"Thanks," she said. She looked at the bridal party, their dresses all a pale blue. The flower girls, Virginia and Megan, looked adorable as they held baskets that contained rose petals. Virginia, with instructions to hang on to Megan, held her little sister's hand. Leah was matron of honor with Allison's closest friends as bridesmaids. Jared had chosen Sloan as best man, with Ryan Delaney and some other friends as groomsmen. But it was the groom who captured Allison's gaze.

"It's time," the wedding planner said. The wedding march began and the guests all stood, turning toward her. She began the slow walk down the aisle. She could see nothing but Jared. Looking incredibly handsome, he stood there quietly, his eyes on her. She smiled as she walked toward him to become his wife. She felt as if she might burst with joy. When her father placed her hand in Jared's, she looked up at the man she was about to marry. He smiled and squeezed her hand lightly.

They repeated vows, said prayers, listened to solos and then Jared slipped a gold band on her finger against the dazzling diamond engagement ring. Finally they were introduced as Mr. and Mrs. Jared Weston. She walked back up the aisle on the arm of her husband.

Afterward at the country club, the reception was filled with guests. Allison stood in a large circle talking to the Delaneys. She barely knew the eldest Delaney couple, William and Ava. They had a beautiful little girl with them, Caroline. Zach and Emma, who was expecting, were with them along with Ryan, looking dashing in his black tux and black boots. Garrett and Sophia Cantrell were there, too, and Allison knew Sophia was a Delaney. Jared seemed to be enjoying the conversation, but occasionally he would glance at her, and then she felt shut away with him, as if the crowd had ceased to exist.

Later she danced with Ryan who smiled at her. "Jared told me he's giving up bull riding. I suspect I have you to thank for clearing the way for me to win a little more often than I have in the past."

She laughed. "You're welcome. You might not owe me that thank-you, though. It was getting time he quit anyway."

"Suits me just fine. You look beautiful, Mrs. Weston."

"Thank you."

"And Jared looks happier than I've ever seen him look. I wish both of you the best."

"Another thank you, Ryan."

The dance ended, and she turned to see Phillip approaching. As Ryan left, Phillip stepped up. "So may I have this dance?"

"Of course. I saw you at your table but haven't had a chance to speak to you," she said, dancing with him.

"I congratulated Jared. You look beautiful today."

"Thank you, Phillip. Did you bring a guest with you?"

His smile widened. "I did. Her name is Ginger, and I want you to meet her. Allison, I think it was better for both of us that you never accepted my marriage proposals. We might have had a wonderful union, but you're radiant today. One look at you and Jared and there's no question you have so much more than you and I would have had. And I think I may have found someone."

"I'm glad, Phillip."

She danced with him and when the dance ended, Jared appeared to take her into his arms. "You are the most beautiful bride ever."

"I doubt you've paid any attention to brides in the past," she said, laughing.

"Maybe not, but you are definitely the most beautiful."

As they danced away, she told him, "Jared, Phillip has found someone, too. He said it was best for both of us that I never accepted."

"I have to agree with him." Jared spun her in time to the music. "I see your brother watching us. Has he danced with you yet?"

"Not yet."

"I think that's what's on his mind. He'll feel obligated.

Since Sloan got married, he has all these family things he thinks he should do. I hope my new brother-in-law doesn't drive me crazy."

"You've known him all your life, and he's not going to really be very different."

"How long before we can leave and I can have you all to myself?"

"I'd say maybe three hours."

"Seriously? I may grab you and run before three hours are up."

She smiled. "I don't think there will be any resistance on my part."

"Aah, that's my Allison." The dance ended. "Here he comes. And be ready—we'll make a run for it in another hour."

"Hour and a half would be halfway respectful and friendly to our guests."

"It's a date, darlin'. I'm counting the minutes, Mrs. Weston."

"Jared, I love you."

He winked at her and turned to Sloan. "My new brother-in-law. If I had thought I was getting you for a relative in this deal, I might not have gone through with it."

"Don't kid me. It's one of the perks for you. Now you won't have to pay me a commission on deals I find for you."

"I didn't think of that. Maybe that will offset having to put up with you and your worrying."

"I worried you two into marriage, so be grateful. I came to dance with my sister."

She smiled and took his hand. "I don't think we've done this since I was about five years old. That was the last time you were nice to me when we were kids. By the time I was six, you were already giving me grief."

Sloan laughed as they both joined the other people dancing.

It was almost an hour and a half later when Allison couldn't spot Jared in the main ballroom. She walked around, talking to guests. As she passed a door to the hallway, she felt a hand reach in and circle her wrist. Smiling she stepped into the hall.

"Let's go," Jared said, a devilish smile on his face.

"I haven't tossed my bridal bouquet."

"I told Sloan to get Leah to throw it. She was matron of honor, so she's the next best thing." He took the bouquet and placed it on a chair. "She'll find it."

Laughing, Allison took his hand and they raced outside, climbing into a waiting limo that had the motor running.

As they drove away, he closed the partition between them and the driver, and then pulled her into his arms to kiss her.


Later that night, they entered a villa in the Cayman Islands. He carried her over the threshold and set her on her feet.

"It's beautiful here," she said, gazing up at him.

"The most gorgeous view in the world is right here," he said, smiling at her. "Allison, you've made me the happiest man in the world. Why did I ever think I wanted to spend my time struggling up a frozen mountain instead of being with you? You were right."

"I'm glad you feel that way, and I hope you always do. I'll just try to avoid watching some of the scary things you do."

"In the meantime, I have some other activities in mind. Ah, darlin', I love you."

"And I love you, my handsome husband," she said, wrapping her arms around his neck and standing on tiptoe to kiss him. Joy spread throughout her, and she felt filled to overflowing with love for her new husband. "Jared," she whispered, "may our life together always be this grand and our love stronger as the years go by."

"Darlin', I love you with my whole heart."

Joyously she returned to kissing him, blissful in her hours-old marriage, loving this wonderful man who had vowed to love her.

\* \* \* \* \*

*If you loved Jared and Allison's story,*
*don't miss a single novel in*
LONE STAR LEGACY,
*a Texas-set series from*
USA TODAY *bestselling author Sara Orwig:*

*RELENTLESS PURSUIT*
*THE RELUCTANT HEIRESS*
*MIDNIGHT UNDER THE MISTLETOE*
*ONE TEXAS NIGHT...*

*All available now from Harlequin Desire!*

# COMING NEXT MONTH FROM

◆ **HARLEQUIN**®

## *Desire*

### Available November 5, 2013

## #2263 THE SECRET HEIR OF SUNSET RANCH
*The Slades of Sunset Ranch* • by Charlene Sands
Rancher Justin Slade returns from war a hero...and finds out he's a father. But as things with his former fling heat back up, he must keep their child's paternity secret—someone's life depends on it.

## #2264 TO TAME A COWBOY
*Texas Cattleman's Club: The Missing Mogul*
by Jules Bennett
When rodeo star Ryan Grant decides to hang up his spurs and settle down, he resolves to wrangle the heart of his childhood friend. But will she let herself be caught by this untamable cowboy?

## #2265 CLAIMING HIS OWN
*Billionaires and Babies* • by Olivia Gates
Russian tycoon Maksim refuses to become like his abusive father, so he leaves the woman he loves and their son. But now he's returned a changed man...ready to stake his claim.

## #2266 ONE TEXAS NIGHT...
*Lone Star Legacy* • by Sara Orwig
After a forbidden night of passion with his best friend's sister, Jared Weston gets a second chance. But can this risk taker convince the cautious Allison to risk it all on him?

## #2267 EXPECTING A BOLTON BABY
*The Bolton Brothers* • by Sarah M. Anderson
One night with his investor's daughter shouldn't have led to more, but when she announces she's pregnant, real estate mogul Bobby Bolton must decide what's more important—family or money.

## #2268 THE PREGNANCY PLOT
by Paula Roe
AJ wants a baby, and her ex is the perfect donor. But their simple baby plan turns complicated when Matt decides he wants a second chance with the one who got away!

---

**YOU CAN FIND MORE INFORMATION ON UPCOMING HARLEQUIN® TITLES, FREE EXCERPTS AND MORE AT WWW.HARLEQUIN.COM.**

HDCNM1013

# REQUEST YOUR FREE BOOKS!
## 2 FREE NOVELS PLUS 2 FREE GIFTS!

**H HARLEQUIN®**

*Desire*

### ALWAYS POWERFUL, PASSIONATE AND PROVOCATIVE

**YES!** Please send me 2 FREE Harlequin Desire® novels and my 2 FREE gifts (gifts are worth about $10). After receiving them, if I don't wish to receive any more books, I can return the shipping statement marked "cancel." If I don't cancel, I will receive 6 brand-new novels every month and be billed just $4.55 per book in the U.S. or $4.99 per book in Canada. That's a savings of at least 13% off the cover price! It's quite a bargain! Shipping and handling is just 50¢ per book in the U.S. and 75¢ per book in Canada.* I understand that accepting the 2 free books and gifts places me under no obligation to buy anything. I can always return a shipment and cancel at any time. Even if I never buy another book, the two free books and gifts are mine to keep forever.

225/326 HDN F4ZC

Name _____ (PLEASE PRINT) _____

Address _____ Apt. # ____

City _____ State/Prov. _____ Zip/Postal Code _____

Signature (if under 18, a parent or guardian must sign)

Mail to the **Harlequin® Reader Service:**

**IN U.S.A.:** P.O. Box 1867, Buffalo, NY 14240-1867
**IN CANADA:** P.O. Box 609, Fort Erie, Ontario L2A 5X3

**Want to try two free books from another line?**
**Call 1-800-873-8635 or visit www.ReaderService.com.**

* Terms and prices subject to change without notice. Prices do not include applicable taxes. Sales tax applicable in N.Y. Canadian residents will be charged applicable taxes. Offer not valid in Quebec. This offer is limited to one order per household. Not valid for current subscribers to Harlequin Desire books. All orders subject to credit approval. Credit or debit balances in a customer's account(s) may be offset by any other outstanding balance owed by or to the customer. Please allow 4 to 6 weeks for delivery. Offer available while quantities last.

**Your Privacy**—The Harlequin® Reader Service is committed to protecting your privacy. Our Privacy Policy is available online at www.ReaderService.com or upon request from the Harlequin Reader Service.

We make a portion of our mailing list available to reputable third parties that offer products we believe may interest you. If you prefer that we not exchange your name with third parties, or if you wish to clarify or modify your communication preferences, please visit us at www.ReaderService.com/consumerschoice or write to us at Harlequin Reader Service Preference Service, P.O. Box 9062, Buffalo, NY 14269. Include your complete name and address.

HDI3R

**P**hoebe opened her front door with some trepidation. Not because she had anything to fear from the man on the porch. She'd been expecting him for several hours. What she dreaded was telling him the truth.

She backed up, and he entered, sucking all the air out of the room. He was a big man, built like a lumberjack, broad through the shoulders, and tall. His thick, wavy chestnut hair gleamed with health. The glow from the fire that crackled in the hearth picked out strands of dark gold.

When he removed his jacket, she saw that he wore a deep blue sweater along with dark dress pants. The faint whiff of his aftershave mixed with the unmistakable scent of the outdoors. He filled the room with his presence.

Reaching around him gingerly, she flipped on the overhead light, sighing inwardly in relief when the intimacy of firelight gave way to a less cozy atmosphere.

He gave her home a cursory glance, then settled his sharp gaze on her face. His masculine features were put together in a pleasing fashion, but the overall impression was intensely male. Strong nose, noble forehead, chiseled jaw, and lips made for kissing a woman.

His scowl grew deeper. "I'm tired as hell, and I'm starving. If you could point me to my cabin, I'd like to get settled for the night, Ms....?"

"Kemper. Phoebe Kemper. You can call me Phoebe." Oh, wow. His voice, low and gravelly, stroked over her frazzled nerves like a lover's caress. The faint Georgia drawl did nothing to disguise the hint of command. This was a man accustomed to calling the shots.

She swallowed, rubbing damp palms on her thighs. "I have a pot of vegetable beef stew still warm on the stove. You're welcome to have some."

The aura of disgruntlement he wore faded a bit, replaced by a rueful smile. "That sounds wonderful."

She waved a hand. "Bathroom's down the hall. I'll get everything on the table."

"And afterward you'll show me my lodgings?"

Gulp. "Of course."

He was most likely going to be furious with her, no matter how she tried to spin the facts.

Because his lodgings had been destroyed in the storm and the only bed left for miles was in this cabin—with her.

*Don't miss*

*A BILLIONAIRE FOR CHRISTMAS*

*Available December 2013 from Harlequin Desire!*